HOLLOW SKULLS

AND OTHER STORIES

SAMUEL MARZIOLI

JOURNALSTONE
YOUR LINK TO ARTIST TALENT

ISBN: 978-1-950305-56-8 (sc)
ISBN: 978-1-950305-57-5 (ebook)

First printing edition: January 8, 2021
Published by JournalStone Publishing in the United States of America.
Cover Design and Layout: Don Noble
Edited by Sean Leonard
Proofreading and Interior Layout by Scarlett R. Algee

JournalStone Publishing
3205 Sassafras Trail
Carbondale, Illinois 62901

JournalStone books may be ordered through booksellers or by contacting:
JournalStone | www.journalstone.com

To Olivia, Chloe, Roy, Joanne, Sarah, Nick, Isaac, and Tracey. I couldn't have asked for a better, more supportive family.

CONTENTS

HOLLOW SKULLS

AND OTHER STORIES

A POCKET OF MADNESS

GENER STUMBLED NAKED THROUGH his back yard, his breath streaming through his teeth in cotton wisps. The moon was absent, and the stars shone an angry shade of red as if their light had been distilled through the meat of someone's palm. With the streetlamps off, he couldn't see beyond the boundaries of his property. But he didn't care, wouldn't stop; he had to keep on searching.

Once he reached the center of his yard he kneeled, scrabbling through a layer of grass and shallow roots. He pressed his ear against the cold, damp earth. A faint rumble sounded deep below, growing louder as the source of the disturbance strengthened, sending soft vibrations through his skull.

It's coming, he thought. *It's coming and no one knows but me.*

He woke the next morning still naked, his hands and feet streaked with mud and dirt. The fact he had sleepwalked didn't bother him as much as the feeling that the world had gone wrong, like the madness of an Escher-scape with all its defects and illusions. He told his wife Cathy about it while they finished breakfast at the kitchen table. Not that he had another episode, just the abnormalities he'd felt when he awoke.

"Honey," Cathy said, in that patient tone she used whenever their daughter Rachel was upset. "Remember how you were when we moved in together, or when you quit your job and started your home business? Not to mention the way you acted when Rachel was conceived."

His breath caught, and he transferred scolding eyes from her to Rachel in the living room. Rachel was rolling on the carpet amid stacks of still-sealed moving boxes and furniture gathered in a cluster. Their eyes locked. She waved and he waved back, feigning a smile.

"That was low," he muttered.

"It wasn't meant to be," she said, and took him by the wrist. "All I'm saying is you don't like change, and ever since we started moving, change is all you've had. Once we settle in, I mean truly organize this clutter, I have no doubt you'll feel better."

He fought the impulse to snatch his hand away, to free himself from the feel of scouring pads rubbing his skin raw.

"Yeah. Maybe you're right," he said, but he couldn't bring himself to believe it.

* * *

They spent the remainder of the day shuffling their belongings up and down the stairs, assigning essentials to drawers and closet space, and organizing the furniture. The following day was Rachel's birthday. While their two-week move had been exacting, they managed to assemble the bones of a party plan while lying in bed that night.

The next morning, Cathy woke Rachel early and took her on the pretense of a girls' day out. Gener stayed behind to decorate. He wanted the house to be spectacular, chock-full of bright colors and shiny things—whatever it took to help Rachel forget the friends she'd moved away from and would probably never see again. But he had to admit, part of it was to assuage the glacial ache that formed whenever Rachel's birthdays came around.

When Cathy first told him she was pregnant, he wasn't ready to be a father yet. His notion of a baby was a needy gob of flesh that devoured all of space and time around it, like some diminutive black hole. He'd even accused his wife of cheating, based on the razor-thin reason he always used a condom. Even his basic grasp of biology was enough to discredit his suspicions, but his mind had been set to automatic, fueled by insecurities, not evidence and logic.

To his credit, he'd embraced the truth well before his daughter's birth. In time, she became the sunrise of his days and the moonlight of his evenings. He never believed he could feel that way about a child, but the last eight years of fatherhood had proven him many times the liar.

When Rachel burst through the front door—trailed by a tired, plodding Cathy—the trappings had been set. Streamers spanned the house, with mobs of Mylar balloons separated by message and color. Pin-up games of cartoon animals adorned every wall, and noise makers of various shapes and sizes sat in bowls, awaiting a puff of air to bring their voices to life.

"I. Love. It," Rachel said, throwing herself at Gener, and crushing him in a monster hug.

"Looks great," said Cathy. "You really outdid yourself."

The great lump of ice inside Gener melted to a speck. "Anything for my baby girl."

After a few rounds of party games, and running through the sprinklers out back, they reconvened on the living room couch. Gener and Cathy occupied the space on either side of Rachel as she tore through her gifts, her cheeks quivering from the strain of all her smiles. She received several toys, a dozen books, some stuffed animals and—"Last, though I certainly hope not least," said Gener—a hula hoop.

"I've always wanted one of these," Rachel said, holding up the hula hoop. "How did you know?"

"Call it a father's intuition," said Gener. "Do you really like it?"

"Yeah. It's awesome!"

* * *

A month passed before Gener had another episode. This time he wandered through the streets of his new neighborhood, calling Rachel's name. The night dripped darkness thick as candlewax, smothering the world at the borders of his vision. Houses watched him as he passed, silently laughing, as if he were a punch line to a joke he should have known but couldn't quite remember.

When he woke, it felt as if his room had become untethered from the house. A blurred lens filtered out finer details, transforming everything into mere impressions of what they'd been. Bolstered by a wave of panic, he rushed for the hallway, intent on finding Rachel. He didn't notice the bedroom door until he collided with it and crumpled to the floor.

"It's all in my mind," he told himself, staring up as faces in the stucco ceiling rearranged themselves and clarified into meaningless dollops before his eyes. "It isn't real."

His doctor had called his unusual experiences "hypnopompic hallucinations." A sort of augmented reality where gargantuan spiders appeared, vortices opened in thin air, and foreign words pasted themselves to the walls and ceiling like the pages of some ancient tome. With his recent bouts of sleepwalking—what he and Cathy had taken to calling "episodes"—things had only gotten worse. He felt trapped between two storm fronts, fearful of what he might think, or do, or say while his mind was lost in the tumult of their merging.

Kathy had left early in the morning, so Gener tended to his and Rachel's breakfast. Between each earnest bite, Rachel slopped her spoon into her cereal bowl and regaled him with stories of what she'd done so far that summer. Most of her stories involved various "tricks" she'd taught herself—her word for a spastic dance she did while hooping that never failed to remind Gener of someone shaking ants loose from their underwear.

"That's great, honey. I'm so glad you like it," he said.

"I got some new tricks I want to show you."

"Okay, but I've got a lot of work to finish first."

He wasn't done by the allotted time, but he dutifully trudged out back and draped himself across the edge of the deck. Their back yard was a quarter-acre lawn, with a strip of earth separating it from the surrounding fences. A drainage system with an iron grate had been installed where the ground bowled in its center. Rachel had come to love that grate. She used it as a stage. Since her birthday, not a day went by where she didn't drag one or both of her parents out back for an impromptu performance.

"Presenting Rachel, the Hula Hoop Queen!" Rachel announced.

He tried his best to give his full attention, but as each new trick piled on, various projects gamboled through his mind and he could think of nothing else.

"That's all for today, honey."

"Come on, Daddy," Rachel begged. "One last one."

"Save it for next time," he said, rising to his feet.

"It'll only take a second."

"I said no."

"Please? Come on, just one—"

"Goddamn it, Rachel, not right now!"

Rachel went still. Her shoulders slumped in a quiet sulk and her bottom lip bulged between the wet lines of her tears. Gener retreated to the patio. Before he went inside, he meant to apologize, to promise his undivided attention the next time she had a show. But when he turned, the world went still and all sound drained into an eerie silence, save for the wild beating of his heart. Rachel was gone. Only her hula hoop remained, its plastic rim circling the grate like a target on a map.

* * *

When Cathy returned from work, Gener was seated on their backyard deck, picking at the knowledge of Rachel's absence as if it were a fresh scab covering an old wound.

"The house is a mess," she said. "What were you two doing in there?"

He took the barest moment to meet her gaze. Whatever she saw in his expression made her face blanch.

"What is it?" and then, when she caught the measure of his silence, "Where's Rachel?"

His arms felt like dead things, fastened to his shoulders by a twist of string, but he managed a shrug. Cathy rushed inside. Through the open windows, he could hear her scramble through the house, scouring the rooms, ransacking the closets, raking through the disarray he'd left behind as she screamed their daughter's name. When her search proved as fruitless as his had, she came back outside, her eyes and cheeks a mess of dripping, black mascara.

"She can't have gone far. You search by foot and I'll take my car. We'll—"

"No," said Gener, shaking his head. "I tried already, even went knocking door to door. It's useless."

"How can you say that?"

"Because it's true. Didn't I warn you? Didn't I say the world had gone wrong? A pocket of madness opened and swallowed up our daughter. I haven't figured out how or why, but she's still here. Waiting for us to find her."

Something like revulsion brimmed in Cathy's eyes. He knew she wouldn't understand. He barely understood, and he'd been pondering it for hours.

He scanned the back yard one last time, weaving through the mat of drying grass to the iron grate that crowned its center. His suspicions sunk through its slots into the web of black hiding underneath. A sudden chill leeched the warmth from him, and he shivered and turned, seeking refuge in Cathy's face. But there was nothing for him there either except more cold and darkness.

Cathy called the police. When the officer arrived, Gener told her what he knew, though after Cathy's contemptuous reaction he fell short of sharing every detail. The officer searched the house and property, making a point to mention all the things that had made Rachel's disappearance peculiar: the tight, high panels of the fence; the rusted gate lock that wouldn't budge; the shallow catch basin below the grate, with a fist-sized drainpipe underneath.

"She could have climbed out a window," the officer suggested.

"No," said Gener. "She never went inside."

Gener could read her doubt written clear as text across her face. She had her theory—negligent father dozes off—but for Gener, the simple answers had been precluded. In Rachel's last moments, he'd held her reflection, could almost feel her distress bleeding from the glass of the patio door. Though he hadn't recognized the importance at the time, she'd vanished exactly where she'd stood.

* * *

Cathy took Gener on a drive around the city. She grilled him for more information as they took turns shouting their daughter's name out the open windows. He only reiterated what he'd told her before: vague ideas, the details of which still left him grasping at absurdities and shadows. Cathy cried, refused to say another word to him besides, "That's crazy. You're crazy," and, "What's happening to you?"

She dropped to the couch when they got back home, clutching her cellphone to her chest as if it were a lucky talisman. He sat beside her, held her hand.

"We'll find her soon. I promise," he said, the dull echo of the lie thudding through the cavern of their living room.

Night came before Cathy's sobs slipped into the long, deep grooves of sleep. He gave her hand a gentle kiss and then made his way outside. The stars were gone and the moon was a waning crescent. It gave the sky an empty feel, as if the heavens were tired things sliding into the dark side of eternity, and the little globe of Earth lay abandoned in the universe. It felt like too much of a coincidence to not mean something, but he couldn't imagine what.

Lying flat on his belly by the grate, he listened to the doldrums, hoping Rachel's voice would echo from the ground and justify every single word he'd said.

I'll find you, Rachel, he thought, before the early morning came and—with a warm, soft blanket of wind—lulled him into an anxious sleep.

* * *

Rachel stood on the grate, her hula hoop gliding around her waist with the smooth grace of rings orbiting Saturn.

"Watch me, Daddy. Bet you I can reach a thousand!"

"No way! That's a sucker's bet," said Gener, seated on the deck, his chin resting on his upturned hands.

"You're doing great, honey," said another Gener, sprawled out on the ground beside Rachel.

From the second Gener's viewpoint, Rachel's head eclipsed the sun. Its rays gilded her with an aura bright as fire, and he reached through the increasing distance for the silhouette of her face.

"Watch me, Daddy," Rachel said again, but her voice was deeper now, as if time had stalled, pouring her words out slow as dripping batter.

The earth began to crawl, a sluggish shake that pitched both Geners to their backs. They recovered in time to watch as the grate slots parted, transformed into a mouth. Rachel fell inside. The mouth clamped shut around her. Its metal teeth grinded through her flesh and bones, swallowing both her and the guttural screams that followed.

Gener on the deck scrambled on his hands and knees, the shocked ovals of his eyes lingering long after he vanished.

Gener on the ground scurried forward and gazed into the endless gullet of the drainpipe. Far below, something returned his stare. A vile thing cloaked in black, the suggestion of a face split in two by a wide, salacious grin. Gener jolted back before the face receded and the mouth reverted to a harmless grate again.

"What are you doing?"

He hauled himself around to find Cathy gaping at him through a crack in the patio door, dressed in her pajamas.

"I've found Rachel!"

Cathy's strangled moans trailed her across the lawn and she fell to her knees beside Gener.

"She's inside," he said. "Help me pull her out."

Cathy wrenched the grate off and Gener thrust his arms into the catch basin. His fingers squirmed, scraping at the walls, slithering halfway into a drainpipe too slim to admit his bulk. When he withdrew his hands at last, all he had to show for it were two fists full of brown sludge, slick as oil.

Words hovered out of Gener's reach. He licked the dryness from his lips, gazing at Cathy in quiet desperation. She looked too pale to be alive, her face frozen in grief, in shock, in terror.

"Cathy, you have to believe me." He inched forward, reaching out to her, sludge drooling through his splayed fingers. "I saw her. She was there."

Her eyes met his, but they stared blind, devoid of understanding. "Gener," she said, a shrill note of condemnation before she hurried back inside.

* * *

Gener wasn't surprised when Cathy told him she was leaving. The months had grown long teeth and bitter claws between updates from police that never brought good news. Nightly screaming arguments only made things worse, washing over them like an acetone solution, loosening their bonds until they finally slid apart. He could see the change come over her. It was in the way she stroked his face, her coddling inflection, the wet glass of her eyes looking through him to a place full of reminiscing and regret.

"You have every right to fall apart," she said, after she'd packed her things in matching suitcases and stuffed her car with boxes. "But I can barely hold myself together. If I stay, both of us might break and where would that leave Rachel?"

"I am trying to help," he said.

"I know."

"I will find her."

"Okay."

"I'm not crazy."

Her eyebrows furrowed and her lips flattened to a line, but she had no response for that one.

Gener remained in the family home. He drifted soundlessly from room to room, speaking his daughter's name only in sobs and cracking whispers. He spent most of his time holding vigil in the back yard, hoping to fall asleep and find one last glimmer of his daughter in the dust and cobwebs of his brain. But he couldn't sleep, much less dream, and soon the prospect of a hypnopompic visitation felt as vacant as the house.

Unlike Cathy, he never saw the point of taping posters up to windows, or handing flyers out to callous passersby. He much preferred to search the internet, sewing a quilt from disparate information where the borders were all frayed and the pieces didn't fit. Still, some of it proved interesting.

On a personal blog, he read about a man from Gilbertville who'd excavated a swimming pool in his back yard shortly before his wife disappeared. On a forum for sharing paranormal experiences, a woman from Cedar Rapids claimed a hole left from a tree trunk removal had gobbled up her dog. On a website dedicated to missing children, a mother in Eldridge reported last seeing her son while he was digging for buried treasure in a field adjacent to their house.

He sent all three of them an email. A month passed before someone responded.

"Pick my brain, if you think it'll help," the mother from Eldridge wrote. She signed it, simply, "Mary."

The sight of it brought a too-rare smile to Gener's face. In and by itself, her message promised him no answers. But added to the modest pile of what he knew, it felt like hope, a true step forward when all he had was a series of retreats. He wrote her back immediately.

* * *

When Gener pulled his car up to the curb, Mary was waiting on the sidewalk, buried in the shade of her front yard's looming oak. From the look of her, she could have been any suburban mom he'd ever met, with sagging sweats and a food-stained tee that spoke of many mornings hustling breakfast and wrangling kids out to the school bus. But the dark halos around her eyes exposed a different truth: one of sleepless nights, of days spent crying, and the underlying pain of loss that had put a touch of madness in her. He would know. He'd seen that same look from the almost-stranger who watched him from his mirrors.

"Mary?" he said.

"You must be Gener."

"That's me. Are you sure you wouldn't be more comfortable at a restaurant or a coffee shop?"

"This is farther from my house than I prefer to be already."

He nodded and she turned, leading him the several steps to the start of the field beside her house. It was a flat expanse of dirt, acres wide and twice as long. Scattered tufts of weeds added a splash of gold to the russet-colored earth, and a timid tree stood out in the middle like a tourist who'd lost his way and refused to ask directions.

"Over there," Mary said, motioning to the remnants of a hole.

It was smoothed by wind and rain into an ankle-deep impression. Gener stooped before it.

"That's where he was when I last saw him," she said. "I never meant to let him play alone, but his brothers were with my husband, his best friend was sick, and I was so damn tired. I told him, 'Don't you wander off, and stay where I can see you.' As if that helped."

"Anyone else see it happen?" he said, pointing toward the picket fence and the curtained windows of the closest neighbor's house.

"Just me."

He poked at the center of the impression with a finger. "What was going on before he vanished?"

Mary's lips spread in a frown, exposing too many teeth. "He was digging. He must have dug a good two feet deep because I remember thinking how strange it was to see the upper half of him, like a severed torso gliding back and forth. As I explained before, I turned away for a second and the next time I looked up…"

She crossed her arms and shut her mouth, as if holding back a tremble and a blooming need to wail.

"What happened next?" he asked, pinching at the brown sludge sticking to his fingers—the same kind he found beneath the grate back home.

"I ran. I ran and ran and ran. When I got to him, all that was left was a black hole that ran too deep. Miles of it punched into the ground, and in its center…"

She choked, pressed her palm against her mouth and held it.

"Go on," he said, heart pounding, knees trembling from the weight of anticipation. "What did you see?"

He knew the answer before he even asked the question. Different words for brush strokes, a divergent color palette, but still the same image painted on the canvas of his mind. Nevertheless, he had to know, had to hear it for himself.

"I looked down and it looked back, grinning, knowing what it'd done and daring me to stop it. I think a lot about that moment, taking the view from various perspectives, and I always come to one conclusion."

"What's that?"

"Hell isn't a lake of fire. It's a place absent of all warmth and light. That's what I saw. That's where it lives, and that's where it took my son."

* * *

Gener left Eldridge in a better mood—nowhere like elation, but greater than his previous despair. Now that he confirmed the madness was real, he realized his dreams and hallucinations had only heightened his awareness, not hindered it. He wasn't broken. Cathy was wrong. The police were wrong. Only he was right.

For months he'd felt useless, a specter haunting his own house, doomed to repeat the motions of his guilt and grief. Now, when he got home, he surged through every room to reclaim his dominion, pounding on the walls as if they were war drums leading the advancing front.

He prepared another vigil. This time he was armed with a shovel, a wheelbarrow, and the knowledge that irrationality had infested his back yard, its spindly roots burrowed deep into the ground. Anything was possible. Maybe he'd dig enough to penetrate the Earth's outer core of liquid fire. Maybe he'd descend still deeper, carve a tunnel through the center of the planet and come out the other side. But maybe, if luck or chance were with him, he'd pierce the black heart of hell itself and find and save his daughter.

"Rachel," he said, leaning on the shovel's handle as he peered into the grate. Silence ensconced that solitary name, so he continued, "I'm coming for you."

He began to dig, filling the wheelbarrow to its limits before dumping the contents at the farthest corner of his yard. Five feet down and still he kept on digging. Ten feet and the thought of quitting never came. Hours passed; the mound of dirt became a hillock. It was only when he reached twenty feet below the backyard's surface that he dropped at the bottom of the pit, gasping and choking on the salt and tang of earth.

He looked up and saw the eye of the moon squinting down at him. The weight of gravity pinned him to the ground, carving furrows at his edges like the chalk lines of corpses. Numbness spread throughout his body, even as the dirt and rocks and clay absorbed him, dragging him down into a fitful sleep.

* * *

Gener woke the next morning. Red-hot agony threaded through his muscles, the skin of his fingers cracked and wet with ruptured blisters. Like silhouettes thrown across a curtain, he had only a vague sense of what he'd dreamed, but they fueled the maelstrom of his emotions, informed by the failure of last night. Fear, rage, and sadness swimming through his mind in equal portions.

He climbed to his knees. He pressed his shaking hands together, like a swollen steeple in a child's bedtime prayer. "You can take anything you want, anyone you want. You don't need her. Please, give her back."

When that failed to illicit a response, he shouted, "You bastard!" He slammed a hand down, held it against the damp soil. "Show yourself. Meet me face to face, unless you're too much of a coward."

The ground thumped against his palm. The feeling that something unclean had touched him made his skin crawl, and his heart beat to the rhythm of his panicked breaths. Colors muted. Trees faltered. The wind slowed to a pervading calm, and the ground began to shake as if it were alive, a cantankerous beast awakened from its slumber.

Mounds formed along the pit's walls, the outlines of hands quivering underneath their surface, stretching and tearing at the elastic skin of earth. Gener thought of boils forming, of bloated abscesses and maggots swimming in the shallows of a gangrenous infection. He wanted to cover his eyes, to pretend he couldn't see them, but quicker than he could form a plan of disregard, whole arms burst loose and seized him.

"I take it back," he shouted, thrashing, struggling to free himself. "I didn't mean it!"

They threw him down, forcing his face into the dirt. Darkness leaked from the ground like rivulets of oil. Gener could do nothing but watch as the blackness surrounded him, forming tentacles that inched wormlike beneath his clothing, crowding into every crevice, every hole of his body. Once the last of them disappeared inside him, the arms released their grip and slid back into their burrows.

"No more," he said, sobbing at the invasion, the violation. "I'm sorry. No more. I—"

His jaw unhinged with a grinding pop. He screamed unformed words as the muscles of his cheeks tore with the stretching of a smile. Once the line reached from ear to ear, his mouth opened in a face-splitting grin.

"It's not my child."

The words came unwanted, tracing the seams of past transgressions he'd hoped never to remember.

"I never wanted a daughter, much less to be a father."

And then chanting, sobbing, cackling all at once, "Goddamn it, Rachel, not right now! Goddamn it, Rachel, not right now!"

The screech of wheels and the blare of horns confronted him. It wrenched his attention to a clear view of the almost collision in the street. When he turned back again, he found himself sprawled out on the lawn. No hillock of dirt, no signs of excavation. Only narrow holes riddled the back yard—but whether proof of the existence of the arms, or something he had dug himself, he couldn't force himself to make it matter. Like eyes, the holes watched him as he staggered toward the patio. Like mouths, they formed silent taunts and mockeries. After he went inside, they laughed as he closed the door and sealed himself into the quiet condemnation of his house.

* * *

Gener paced the hallway, shivering despite stifling heat blasting from a corner vent. He was too aware of the silence that surrounded him, a mass that spread out along the walls like a parasite of broken homes. Once he backtracked to the entryway again, he clenched his hands and screamed, letting the sound dry into a gurgle.

He continued pacing.

"Hi, Cathy," he muttered. "You'll never believe what happened. They found Rachel and she's alive. Come quickly."

He shook his head, scowling at the cruelty of the suggestion.

"Hi, Cathy. I know this will be hard to believe, but I know how to get Rachel back. At least, I have a plan. Come meet me at the house."

He shook his head again, juggling the mental weight of every word to strike a perfect balance.

"Hi, Cathy. It's Gener. I have something to tell you. Please, come over. It's not the kind of thing that should be said over the phone."

This time he nodded, satisfied. Ever since the morning, he'd kept his mind secret even from himself, not wanting to complicate the process with emotions or the risk of second thoughts. All he allowed himself to know was that he needed her.

He pulled his cellphone from his pocket and dialed. The phone trilled three times before the line picked up.

"Hello?"

"Hi, Cathy? It's me."

* * *

Gener sat on Rachel's bed as he waited for Cathy's arrival, making lazy turns with the hula hoop clutched in his hands. Thoughts crowded in, unfolding in bursts of happy memories. The day he and Cathy met. The day they got married. The day Rachel was born and he held her for the first time. He savored the sweet taste of them, and wept at the failure of his thoughts and actions that had marred so much of his family's fleeting time together.

As soon as Cathy's key jingled in the front door lock, he went to greet her. He risked a smile, but it soon withered when she countered with a grimace, an expression so much like condescension in that insufficient light.

"You look exhausted," she said. "Are you still having episodes?"

"No."

"Hallucinations, then?"

"No. These days, I haven't slept enough to have either one." He meant it as a joke of sorts, but his weak laughter only seemed to rattle her. "I'm glad you came."

"I almost didn't."

"Why?"

"The sound of your voice over the phone. It was different. Not like you at all."

He gave no explanation, just shrugged and cut a path to the patio door. She didn't follow until he beckoned, and even then only after she scanned the clutter of the house: garbage overflowing trash bins, dirty clothes left in slapdash piles, a monolith of unwashed dishes filling up the sink. The sorry state of the back yard only deepened her hesitation. Her eyes skimmed and stumbled over every hole as if puzzling out their meaning, their purpose.

"Gener, why am I here?" she asked.

He didn't have the words to make sense of all his thoughts. The last time they had spoken, Cathy told him she didn't understand him anymore. He supposed part of him wanted to explain himself, to let her know that everything he had done was always about their daughter. Always.

"You remember what I said about how Rachel disappeared? I didn't tell you the whole truth."

He held out a hand, inviting her to take it. She made only a small step forward, skirting the edge of the deck.

"I was where you are now and she was over there," he said, pointing to the grate. "I needed to get back to project plans and deadlines, but she kept begging me to stay. 'One more time, Daddy.' She only wanted to make me proud, and I—"

"What are you trying to tell me? What did you *do?*"

"I yelled at her. No, worse than that, I swore and hurt her with my words." He headed for the center of the lawn, clearing the grate in a single stride. "Ever since then, I've wondered what would have happened if I had put my work aside and watched her play. What would have been the harm in ten more minutes? Maybe she wouldn't have gone missing. Maybe you and I would still be together."

"Is that what this is about?" She shook her head. "A moment of anger didn't take away our daughter. It's not your fault."

"Isn't it?" he said, averting his eyes to the shadows of the grate.

She rushed at him, arms wide with the promise of an embrace. For a moment, he almost let her, longed to feel her liquid warmth after so many months of drought. But the moment passed as soon as she stepped on the grate, and he held his hand out to stop her.

"This isn't about me." His stomach churned. "Don't you see? I can't let that be the last memory Rachel has of her father. I need to make things right."

"What more can you do than what has been tried already?"

"That's just it. You can't say we've tried everything already because I know I haven't. Last night I wrestled with the darkness and the darkness won. It always wins, always has. It got me thinking: maybe yielding to its rules is the only way to bring her back."

Cathy began to cry. "You're doing it again. You're not making any sense."

"Maybe so. I have no idea if this will work, and I might be as crazy as you think. I guess we'll both find out in a moment."

Gener touched her cheek and mouthed, "I love you." He turned to face the other way, but kept his ears perked for her rebuff, a fresh promise of abandonment. The quiet lingered behind him like an accusation, crushing him with guilt. The guessing proved too much to bear, so he turned around again.

Cathy wasn't there.

"Please," Gener said, weeping as he kneeled and pressed his forehead to the ground in supplication. "I have nothing more to offer."

Seconds turned to minutes, minutes turned to hours, but still Rachel didn't reappear. The sun dawdled through the sky, slow as a funeral procession, before weariness and self-loathing consumed him. He closed his eyes. Still clinging to the tatters of hope, he rattled off a sigh and gave himself to the void behind his eyelids.

When he woke the next morning, he found Rachel lying fetal on the grate. Her skin clung to her bones like wet tissue, viscous grime covering her from head to toe. She squinted against the harsh glare of daylight, but remained otherwise inert, didn't seem to realize where she was. With everything that had happened, Gener didn't have the will or strength to laugh or celebrate. He simply scooped Rachel into his arms and wept.

* * *

The police began another search, this time for Cathy. Gener and Rachel were forced to live in their house for the duration of the new investigation. Gener took precautions to make sure Rachel never touched that infected backyard ground again. He ripped the catch basin and drainpipe out, filled the back yard with cement, and even melted the grate into a useless lump of iron.

Rachel was never the same. Sometimes she liked to make divots and stand above them, clapping her fingers to her palm at Gener as if to wave goodbye. Sometimes she lingered over bathtub, sink, and storm drains and scowled into them, as if a face that only she could see were in them, staring out. She didn't speak and rarely moved, even when they relocated across the country. That is, unless she

A POCKET OF MADNESS

was playing with her hula hoop. It was the only time a spark of life returned, shining bright behind the dull, dry roundness of her eyes.

"Watch me, Daddy," she still liked to say on those occasions.

And he did. Despite the passing decades. Despite her auburn hair fading into gray, and the soft, pink roundness of her cheeks sagging into lines. He always did.

BEHIND THE WALLS

WHILE HIS SUBLESSOR JASON boasted of Strossville's tranquility, Coen never imagined how literal that would be. Houses on his block lingered with the tenacity of boulders. Trees and assorted greenery idled like the contents of a photograph, or a movie left on pause. Not to mention the oppressive quiet: no birds chirped, no squirrels chattered, and not a single dog acknowledged Coen's presence even with a stray bark.

After taking a deep breath of suburban air, Coen unpacked his possessions from his car. He didn't bring a lot, since a two-door Bimmer only held so much. Before he'd left home, his parents offered him a moving crew and as much furniture as he wanted. He'd declined. Their help inevitably came with strings attached, and they always got their payback one way or another. Besides, his wanderlust required that he go at it alone. All his life he had everything he wanted, but it felt liberating to start from scratch, and fill in the gaps of ownership one possession at a time.

Once he arranged a few stacks of movies and books and hung his clothes in closets, he settled at the folding desk in the living room and watched a movie on his laptop. Halfway through, a knock sounded from somewhere overhead. Coen shrugged, imagining birds pecking at the rooftop for insects that had burrowed into the age-old grime between the shingles. Never mind he hadn't actually seen any birds in town; they were as ubiquitous as—

"Cats," he said, turning toward the sliding patio door.

A cat stood on its hind legs, resting its front paws against the screen to peer inside. Sunlight seemed to fall around its dense, black fur, never on it. Its ample size and prodigious claws suggested an exotic species, the kind one might expect to see in nature documentaries, draped over a branch in the Amazon or loping through the plains of the Serengeti. But the way it stared at Coen—with a soft, expectant twinkle in its eyes—reminded him of an ordinary house pet.

It pawed the screen, shredding stripes into the mesh. While Jason was technically responsible for any damage, Coen felt the weight of responsibility nonetheless.

"Shoo! Scat!" he shouted, whipping his arms around and rushing at the animal.

The cat purred, soft yet powerful. He could easily imagine that sound rising to the decibels of a lion's piercing roar. One thing was certain: there was nothing ordinary about it.

* * *

Several days passed before Coen called Jason to update him on the progress of his move.

"I'm all settled in," Coen said, lazing on a thrift store couch, a cheap fan from the local hardware store blowing tepid air into his face. "I also sent a money order for this month's rent."

"Thanks, man," said Jason. "I appreciate it. Now remember: act like a home-grown citizen. They don't take too kindly to strangers in Strossville, but more importantly the landlord might sue my ass if she ever found out about our arrangement."

"Shouldn't be hard. I'm a homebody."

"Great. How are things going with that other part of our agreement?"

"I checked a few private animal shelters and rescues in the area. No luck yet."

"Those cats are a local species domesticated by the first settlers. The town has an active breeding program made available specifically for citizens. If worse comes to worst, I can always swing by and pick one up for you."

"Sure, but I'm still not clear on why you care so much if I own one."

"If you didn't believe what I said about Strossville, you sure as hell won't believe me about this."

Coen thought back to the night when they'd first met. It was at some no-name roadside bar, the last oasis before the highway punched through a hundred-mile stretch of desert. Their whisky-fueled exchange made for lively conversation. It was there Coen first learned about Strossville, a closed community swaddled by the wilds of a federal preserve. "It's haunted," Jason said, earnest though far from sober, before recounting stories his parents used to tell him about "the things that live in its dark, hidden spaces."

Regardless of how ridiculous those tall tales sounded, Coen had to see it for himself. Not just because his parents would have hated the idea of him acting so recklessly. Meeting Jason had provided a destination and a purpose to Coen's ill-planned move. He hated to call it fate, but no other term fit so cleanly.

"I believe my exact response was, 'What a bunch of campfire horseshit,'" said Coen, an embarrassed smile gumming up his words.

Jason laughed. "That's right. Let's call this more of that and let it ride."

* * *

Though Coen loved his new place, the unrelenting quiet unsettled him, as if he weren't simply living on his own but was abandoned there. After the first week, he knew there were no immediate neighbors. Not once had a car pulled into a driveway, or slipped from a garage, or parked along the sidewalk within his block. No interior lights ever shone, no matter the time of day, just the same old vacant homes with empty windows staring black. In other words, the town had achieved tranquility, but at the slim cost of absence.

Coen went for a walk at half past seven in the evening, intent on discovering more about his little town. It startled him how pristine everything appeared: the spotless streets and sidewalks, the perfect red and yellow lines painted on curbsides, and the quaint houses that looked like they'd been plucked from a 1950s issue of *Better Homes and Gardens*. His parents would have hated its modest uniformity. He could almost hear his father's voice, passing judgment: "It should be burned, and the ground beneath it salted over." If anything, that only made Coen love it more.

On the next block, a few porch lamps lit front stoops. Through the bay window of one particular house, he spied a couple conversing at their dinner table, and absorbed the sight of them the same way one might bask in the heat of a campfire for warmth. He intended to move on, to explore another part of town, when the couple noticed his intrusive stare and replied with matching frowns. He waved and smiled, trying to evince an air of neighborly politeness. Then he feigned interest in the surrounding houses, as if admiring the architecture or landscaping.

The man rose to his feet and pointed an accusing finger at Coen. Coen looked around and, seeing no one, gestured to himself.

Me? he mouthed.

The man gritted his teeth and shook his head, and the woman jabbed a finger at the glass. Only then did Coen think to turn around. Within the vacant interior of the house behind him, a shadow passed between a wide gap in the curtains. It happened so fast, he couldn't tell its size or shape, and only gleaned a vague notion that the shadow's source had noticed him, was watching him even now.

"Careful, son. Looks like one got loose," the man called out. The couple now stood on their porch, the man's arms folded, and the woman's hands clinging to her hips. "Not the first time either. Have half a mind to sic Bertha on 'em, but the city doesn't want a mess if there's no one there to clean it up."

Coen blinked, and that was all he could think to do. Surely Bertha wasn't this woman, his wife, but with her bulldog scowl and no one else in sight, he couldn't rule it out.

The woman narrowed an eye. "Where's *your* cat? Wandering close, I hope."

"No. I left it at home."

"It's late, son. Since you don't have your cat, it's best to be inside now."

"Your parents should have taught you that already," the woman said, her acerbic tone like wisdom wasted on a fool.

"I forgot, but you can bet my mom would kill me if she ever found out."

He barely suppressed the need to smirk. In truth, his mother hated pets, would have never condoned him owning one, much less dragging one in public. He turned and hurried back the way he came. A few doors down, he threw a glance behind him in time to see the couple filing back into their house. At their window, an orange tabby—big as the stray that frequented his patio—leaned meaty paws against the glass. It fixed its attention on the house where he'd sensed the shadow, eyes big and round and anxious, tail thrashing like a whip.

* * *

The stray cat returned to Coen's patio that night. This time, it wasn't alone. In its mouth it held a gray mass with fur slicked down by blood and a knot of red and purple thumping like a heartbeat from its side. Absent face and limbs, Coen couldn't decipher what the ball of wet and pulsing flesh had been, and considering its state, he wasn't sure he wanted to.

The first several times the cat visited, Coen found it easy to shut his blinds and ignore it. But after his conversations with Jason, he felt obliged to make a greater effort to be friends. Once the glass door slid open, he pulled the screen aside. The cat dropped its prize on the stoop and sat on its haunches, chest puffed up in pride.

Coen went down onto his hands and knees and leaned out the door, his finger hovering over the bleeding mass, impelled to touch it. "What is that?"

The cat meowed, rose to its feet, and pranced boldly through the gap he'd left in the doorway, as if the whole scene was a matter of formality and it was always meant to come inside. As it passed Coen, their eyes met. The cat's lids flared and its pupils narrowed, a violent, bestial stare that turned Coen's arms and legs to mush. He fell forward, almost squishing the cat's offering as it smeared itself along the stoop, a stripe of blood trailing behind it.

"Wait! You can't come in here!"

But he was wrong, and he knew it. He remembered a joke his father liked to tell when he was young: "Where does an 800-pound gorilla sit? Anywhere it wants." Likewise, considering this cat's sheer size, muscles that flexed and bulged under a thick blanket of fur, it could pretty much get away with anything.

It circled the living room, passed into the kitchen and then the downstairs bathroom, before it halted at the board sealing up the staircase spandrel. A knock resounded from the other side, and something scraped along the width of it. Coen jumped back. He tilted his head in the direction of the sound and listened. New neighbors in the adjacent townhouse? Maybe, but he couldn't make himself believe the comfort of that lie.

Silence overtook the house. The cat let out a frantic yowl, clawing at the board, carving divots in the wood. Coen was too stunned to intercede. He remembered the time his parents showed him the family mausoleum, and the fear he felt when imagining the bones and rot concealed within its marble tombs. For a moment, he wondered if his walls concealed something similar, or worse.

Things that live in its dark, hidden spaces.

"No," he said, shaking his head to dispel the thought. His parents weren't the type to fill his mind with absurdities like ghosts and goblins, and he wasn't about to believe in them now.

* * *

The scratching behind the walls intensified. Sometimes a sudden thump cracked the drywall and the pungent scent of mold or rot seeped through. Sometimes the whisper of a squeal emanated from the spandrel. The disturbances persisted for a week, and Coen couldn't take it any longer. To escape the noise, and his growing unease, he took a walk through town and settled in the park, to waste an afternoon watching the scant few passersby.

While there, he called his parents for the first time since he'd left home. They offered him all manner of incentives to return: a new car, an unlimited line of credit, even his own house. When that failed to sway him, they resorted to guilt delivered with blatant aggression, and reiterated threats that they would cut him from their will. The last thing his father said before hanging up was, "You'll be back. You can't survive without us."

Come early evening, Coen stopped by the local grocery store on his way home. The teenage clerks—a boy with a pierced septum and a girl with bleached-blonde hair—stiffened when he stepped through the automatic doors.

"Pet supplies?" he asked.

The girl pointed to the center aisle. When Coen started in that direction, she whispered in the boy's ear. Coen couldn't hear what she said, but could read her body language clear enough: nervousness, and maybe a hint of irritation. Did they know he wasn't local, or was it something else?

After grabbing a bag of cat food, he made a beeline to the freezers for a stack of frozen meals. On the way to checkout, he noticed a metal screen with a staggered diamond pattern bolted over a gash within the outer wall. A few sunbeams streamed through like an array of mini-spotlights illuminating scattered dust and a Strossville cat. The cat concentrated on the screen—its hackles raised and tail bristling—barely giving Coen any attention as he skirted past.

"What happened here?" he called out.

The clerks conferred in muted voices, and then tripped over one another to answer both at once: "Nothing."

He ambled to the front and dropped his items on the counter. "So the wall broke itself?"

"One of those—" the girl began before the boy cut in, "Owners are doing some improvements," he said, giving the girl a not-so-subtle elbow to the ribs.

"Like a window?"

The boy shrugged. "Sure."

Coen shook his head and peeled a fifty from his billfold, content to let the matter rest. "I almost forgot. What aisle are your traps on? I didn't notice any."

"What do you need those for?" asked the girl.

"I think I got an animal of some kind nesting in my walls."

The boy brandished a knowing smirk. "See, I knew you didn't live around these parts."

"Why do you say that?"

"Because. Anyone from Strossville knows we don't carry traps. Not for mice, or rats, or anything."

"Why the hell not?" said Coen, offended by the smugness of the answer.

"No one needs them, so we don't sell them. Simple as that."

* * *

Coen fed his backyard visitor every day. Whenever it appeared with a hunk of unknown meat in tow, he'd grab a cup of kibble and meet it on his patio. They'd exchange offerings and Coen would stroke the cat's fur until it ate its fill. For the one-month anniversary of the day they met, Coen staged a celebration in his living room. He invited the cat inside, went down on a knee, and presented it with a catnip toy, a food dish, and a plush fleece bed.

"We've been seeing each other for a while now," said Coen, as the cat gave its new belongings a perfunctory sniff. "For you, it may be no big deal. You're a cat-about-town; you've probably been with your fair share of humans. But for me, this is new. My parents would have sooner bought and exterminated a whole shelter before they'd let me adopt a pet.

"To mark the occasion, I'm going to stop calling you 'hey' or 'you' or even 'cat.' From now on, you're Strauss."

Strauss didn't seem to care much for the gifts, or Coen's pronouncement. It circled Coen, rubbing against him, craning to reach his hands or bunt his neck and face. They spent the rest of the day reclining on the couch. Coen watched movies while Strauss slept on his lap, spilling the majority of its body over the sides of him. He didn't let it sleep inside overnight, though. Night was the only time the house was still and quiet, and he could be alone with thoughts and future plans that were finally his own.

* * *

Coen slept like a corpse. That's the term he used for the uninterrupted bedtime bliss he'd found in his new home, a solid stretch that lasted until sunup. He looked forward to it, considered it one of the best parts of his days.

With the lamps off, the house was taken over by a rustic dark. He had finished his bedtime routine and eased under the bedspread when knocking started from some far-off wall, presumably downstairs. A minute, and it changed course, drifted closer. Once it reached his bedroom, it changed into a soft patter, as of a dozen tiny feet scampering over the flipside of the ceiling. He fixed his eyes on the commotion, but didn't dare move as it worked its way around the room and then transferred to the walls, pausing in short intervals before resuming its frantic pace.

One more loop, and the sound grew closer, louder. It stopped above his headboard before the gnawing began—loud cracks and shredding wood, as if some thing or things were ripping through the house's frame inches at a time. A deep sweat developed on his forehead.

"Stop it," he whispered, shaking more and more as the din increased, thinning the gap between them.

"I said stop!" Coen shouted, and pounded at the wall, hoping to scare the thing or things away.

A portion of the drywall crumbled beneath his hand, revealing a hole six inches in diameter. Something inside peered out. It scanned the room with moist, red eyes before focusing on Coen, taking him in with a steady, hungry glare. Coen jolted back, smothered his mouth with his hands. Even when the eyes slid away, and the hole resolved to harmless black again, he watched that space, hypnotized by what he'd seen and what it meant.

* * *

"Hello?"

Coen cupped a hand around his phone, hoping it would amplify his whispers. "What's going on here, Jason?"

"Coen? Are you okay? What's wrong?"

"Some *thing* is living in my walls is what's wrong."

"I don't believe it. You actually *saw* something?"

Coen glanced around, sure that his voice would attract the attention of what was hiding in the house's cavities. But when he heard and saw nothing, he relaxed, pressed his back against the glass pane of the patio door.

"Yeah, I saw something. It saw me too. I want to move. You can keep my stuff. I just want out of this place, out of this town, and out of our deal."

"Calm down."

"No, I don't think I will. Now I know why I never see any wild animals in town. Because goddamn monsters in the walls probably ate them."

"Did you get a cat? I told you to get a cat."

"Yes, I got a cat, not that it matters."

"It matters."

"Why? What the hell was watching me, Jason?"

"Some people call them feeders, an apex predator akin to a cougar or bear. A 19th century fur trader named Ivan Kuskov even claimed to have caught one and worn its skin as a trophy. But others say they're altogether different, monsters beyond anything the world has ever seen. There's only one thing everyone agrees upon: they eat anything that's alive."

"And the cats?"

"They're the only things that can hold them back."

* * *

For hours Coen paced the backyard patio, lost in indecision. He almost called his parents and begged them to let him move back home. Then he considered all their rules and stipulations, the inevitable gloating that would follow his return, and all of it tangled in his father's words, "You can't survive on your own," repeating in his mind in endless cycles. Instead, Coen searched the Internet on his phone for other rentals. Somewhere safer, farther north. But once the sun came up, the dread receded along with all the shadows, and he realized he didn't want to leave.

Despite its peculiarities, Strossville had become his home. It was the only place where he had autonomy, and he wasn't about to lose that because he'd gotten a little scared. Besides, if what Jason said was true, the thing in the wall was just an animal wrapped in the mystique of urban legends. Maybe it was dangerous, but so was any carnivore. So long as it breathed and bled, he could kill it.

Coen took a drive to the closest shopping center and picked up a few things in preparation for the night. He bought a leather motorcycle jacket reinforced with metal plates, paintball gloves with PVC armored backing, a 34" aluminum baseball bat, and a catcher's mask with matching leg guards.

On the return drive, he considered the feeder. In his imagination he swapped the details of its body, color, and proportions to match its round and bulbous eyes. At first, it started off a simple thing, no bigger than a possum. But with each subsequent creation, the creature grew larger and more fearsome, a nightmare of claws and fangs that had to wedge the pieces of itself together to fit its bulk within the wall.

"Things that live in its dark, hidden spaces," he muttered, and a shiver skittered down his spine.

He lingered on the patio while he suited up, waiting for Strauss's arrival. The quiet grew intolerable, suffocating. He took to smashing the barrel of his bat against the cement to hear the reassurance of its metallic clink. Every so often, he scanned the surrounding houses, sure that feeders hid behind every window, within every crevice and hole, waiting for the perfect moment to strike. As the day drew to an end, the feeling magnified, until he jumped at every rustling bush or swaying branch.

When Strauss arrived, the cat sauntered through the high grass of the back yard with a bloody ball of viscera in its mouth. Coen looked up into the sky. Already the lilac glow of twilight was draining into black, slender shadows expanding into pools and pillars across the yard. Night was coming fast.

"Ready?" he said to Strauss.

Strauss yawned, dropped the viscera to the ground, and opened the chasm between its jaws.

* * *

No sooner did they step into the townhouse than scratching started up. Now that Coen knew what caused it, the sound took on ominous proportions. He hurried through the downstairs rooms, flipping on lights, while Strauss scanned the ceiling with a patient, rolling stare.

The noise altered to a scrape, a slither, that drifted down the long arm of the hallway toward his bedroom. The shredding of the drywall resumed from last night, but just as Strauss appeared fixed to bolt upstairs, the sound shifted again. A patter of tiny feet merged with heavy dragging as the feeder circled the perimeter of the second floor over and over, as if it were searching for him.

"I'm down here!" Coen shouted, striking the closest wall with his bat.

The feeder fell silent. Was it listening, trying to pinpoint his location? He swallowed hard at the thought, all too aware of exactly how much wall surrounded him, every foot hiding a potential spot for the creature's emergence. Strauss headed to the side of the staircase and paced before the spandrel. Though its hackles raised, and it exposed the daggers of its teeth, it purred.

"Where is it?" Coen muttered, adjusting the catcher's mask over his face. He stepped from the kitchen to the dining room, perking an ear. "Where the hell is it?"

From somewhere distant, the movement resumed. He imagined the feeder rustling through a great expanse of darkness, not simply behind the walls but beyond them. Bestial groans and murmurs emanated from that distant place, each with their own intensity and pitch.

Coen sucked in air as a series of heavy blows landed against the inside of the staircase. The first one shook the wall. The second put a vertical crack into the center of the board, spanning the length of it. The third punched a hole into its upper corner, revealing the feeder's eyes.

An appendage covered in conical protrusions shot into the open. *Fingers*, thought Coen. They were human fingers, each one bent and twitching as they ripped into the board, tearing chunks away. Coen rushed forward and swung the bat with all his might, scattering rows of fingers like twigs knocked loose from soft soil.

"Strauss," he said through gritted teeth. The appendage lengthened, reached for his face. "Help me!"

He heard a choked yowl and glanced down to find Strauss lying on its side, its eyes staring wide and empty.

"Strauss?"

Strauss wouldn't look at him, wouldn't even blink. A small puddle of urine collected between the cat's wide-stretched legs.

At once the fight left him. He turned to run, but the appendage encircled his arm and trapped him in a rigid grip. Hands pushed through the expanded hole, groping at the board's frame, prying at the edges to loosen the nails that held it in place. With one final push, the whole board toppled over, exposing the feeder to the light. The creature swept from the darkness like a cresting wave, its body an amalgam of eyes and mouths, paws and tails, toes, fingers, and heads, all jutting from the surface of the oil slick that was its skin. Its many limbs encircled Coen. He couldn't move, or even scream, before the creature squeezed the breath from him.

Coen thought of his parents, their faces blurred and sparkling like the stars before his eyes. He thought of Strossville and the darkness hidden by its bright façade. Lastly, he thought of Strauss, apparently scared to death by the very thing it was meant to fight. And then, he could think of nothing as the feeder's limbs coiled around him like a serpent, drawing him ever closer to the breach that opened in its torso.

He peered down at his fallen pet. One last look before the end.

A thin line appeared across the side of Strauss's body. The line split apart to reveal the enormous face of a skinned animal, sleek and wet with blood. It dragged its body through the thin flaps of Strauss' hide, paws the size of footballs scrabbling for purchase. When the beast emerged at last, it was a thing of raw, glistening muscle, a hulking mass with the semblance of a cat that loomed over both the feeder and Coen alike.

It loosed a piercing roar. The feeder's grip on Coen slackened and the air rushed back into his lungs, even as the floor rose up to strike his face. The giant beast roared again, and the feeder squealed as if a hundred tiny voices had screamed at once. Coen's world went black.

* * *

He awoke beside a mound of black sludge, and the scattered remains of both human and animal body parts. Blood was smeared into the carpet and spattered on the walls. Sunlight streamed through the open windows. It lit the spandrel beneath the staircase, exposing only a cramped hollow and a water heater fitted snug inside. But nothing else, nothing even remotely like a passageway, or the void that Coen had expected.

He ripped the catcher's mask from his face and searched for the giant beast that had emerged from the cat's body, but found only Strauss: alive and lying on the couch, his furry legs hanging limp over the armrest.

"How? How is this possible?" Coen said, climbing to his hands and knees.

Strauss turned to him and flashed an imperial stare. From somewhere behind its slick black fur and knotted, bulging muscles, it purred.

* * *

Coen lay on the couch with his shirt off, purple bruises thick as ropes wrapped around his arms and chest. He spoke to Jason on the phone for an hour, recounting his experience with the feeder, everything from the moment he uncovered the eyes behind the wall to his discovery the morning after. Once Coen finished, Jason was silent for a good five minutes before a hiss poured through the phone's receiver.

"I feel like I'm to blame," said Jason. "While I grew up with the legends, and even heard a few unexplained noises, I think a part of me never fully believed any of it was true. If I did, I never would have let you live there."

"Don't sweat it," said Coen. "In the end, it was my decision. The important thing is I'm fine."

"Not to make light of your situation, but it makes me glad I moved away. Speaking of which, do you think you'll stick around much longer?"

"I owe Strauss my life and now that I know what he is and what he's meant to do, I can't imagine taking him away—if he'd even let me." He gazed at Strauss, a fat, round blob of fur resting on the tile of the entryway. "So I think I'll stay, at least as long as he wants me around."

"I still can't believe what you told me."

Coen laughed. "It's no big deal, really. You move out of your parents' house, find a place of your own, and then adopt a monster cat to protect you from monsters in the walls. Far as I'm concerned, it's all a part of growing up."

A THING IN ALL MY THINGS

THERE'S A THING IN my closet, crouched in the dark, black lines accentuating every crease and fold of its shriveled face. A cherry-red eye peeks at me. The slash of a frown hints at untold regrets even as its croaking voice spills into the silence.

You should have died in your sleep and saved me all the trouble, it says.

After taking a minute to compose myself, I slip out of bed and hurry past that raw, corrupted space with my eyes averted. In the gloom of the living room, I open the blinds and let the day pour through the slats in glowing strips of light. Breakfast consists of three bowls of cereal and a handful of pills meant—among other things—to squash the thing for good. I unfold the newspaper and try to cloud my brain with random bits of trivia. Stuff the gaps with distractions so that, for one slivered moment, I might forget what's waiting in the other room.

Not that it does a lick of good. For three years it's haunted my life, and there's no rhyme or reason for when or where it will manifest next. A week ago, it appeared hunkered beside me on the porcelain ledge of the bathtub, its eyes staring curses—but only visible through the chrome reflection of the overflow plate. A month ago, it hid beneath my pillow, its fingers worming out from the edges like heavy tongues lapping at the air. Before then, it was behind a hallway air vent, scratching and sobbing inside the living room walls, and on and on, through more days and places than I care to remember.

I head to the bathroom and dawdle through my morning routine: brush my teeth, wash my face, scrub my skin in the shower so it shines the pink of old, healed bruises. But after toweling off, there's no more time to waste. My feet drag across the carpet like dead weights, room to room, until the bedroom closet looms before me.

A chill digs through my skin as I reach into that infected recess. The thing flattens against the wall, like it's pretending to be a shadow or a patch of mold. As if it thinks I can't hear the sound of its spectral lungs pulling in the thought of air. Though I know it will not scratch or bite, it takes some time for me to steady my nerves, assemble my clothes, and prepare for work.

* * *

There's a thing in the espresso maker of my barista station. It fiddles with the inner workings, making the shots burn too hot or steep too thin. Its scalded fingers wiggle from the spouts, deep red filling the gossamer cracks in its broken, bloated skin.

We're slammed at exactly 6 AM. The line of vehicles stretches across the parking lot, like the boxcars of two stalled freight trains. My co-workers scurry around—with a manic intensity that makes the Café Stop's interior feel small as a crypt—and all of them barking orders.

On my best days, I can knock out eighty drinks an hour. But my best days never come when the thing's around. Its blood sprinkles into the milk pitchers, and I have to dump them out in the sink to start again. Its spit dribbles down the espresso spouts, forcing me to remove the portafilters and wash them. It even reaches out from the water reservoir and whacks at finished drinks, upsetting their lids and spilling the contents across the counter.

My boss yells at me for the mess. "Damn it, Tom! If you can't get your shit together, maybe you should find another place to hang your apron, mister!" Like a parent scolding an unruly child. As if I weren't twice his size and hadn't trained him from the day he first stepped through the back door.

I almost say as much, until the thing knocks against the espresso machine's plastic interior. Its whispered taunts, hidden behind the screech of steaming milk, lift stark as any shouted voice: *Can't you do anything right? You're useless. A waste of air.*

It drains the fight from me. I nod, apologize and say, "Sorry, sir. It won't happen again."

* * *

There's a thing in my cigarette lighter. It wets the wire so it can't spark and clogs the jet valve so the butane won't release. Sometimes it sticks its head into the torch stream, infusing my cigarettes with the scent and taste of rotting flesh and burning hair.

My co-worker, Cara, slips out the Café Stop entrance and heads for the dumpster cage where we're forced to spend our smoke breaks. She stands aloof, snatches the cigarette from behind her ear and lights it up. She avoids making eye contact with me, same as everyone on any given day. Because I'm intense, they say, and they sometimes catch me talking to the thing even though I'm the only one who can see and hear it.

"Hi," I say to lighten the mood. Because Cara's one of the good ones—beautiful inside and out—no matter how shy or scared of me she is.

"Hey, Tom." She pauses to take a drag. "Mike's a real asshole for yelling at you like that."

"Yeah," I say.

"Don't let it get to you. He knows you're a good worker, and it's not like he doesn't have his off days, too."

"Maybe."

"Any plans for after work?" she says, examining her shoes like mushrooms just sprouted from the leather.

Now is the perfect time. I take a breath to calm the vicious beating of my heart, assembling words I've rehearsed since the day she and I first met. "Actually, I was wondering if maybe you'd like to—"

But the world around me comes alive, spewing the thing's vocalized disdain. *Lardo*, from the gray smoke leaking from Cara's mouth.

"No."

"No what, Tom?"

Fatty plumpkin, from the burrows insects punched into the dumpster's rotting food.

"Stop it."

"Tom, I'm not saying or doing anything."

Chubby little bastard, from my own shadow wedged beneath

my feet.

"Just go away, goddamn it!" I shout, swatting at the voices crowding in, crawling all around me.

She runs for the café's entrance before I can explain, and I'm left alone. Same as always. It proves too much. Though I've managed to push the rage aside till now, the pressure builds, and my inner parts stretch and tear from the strain. The thing can't hurt me, I tell myself. But I know I'm wrong because it always does and nothing—not therapists, doctors, or even pills—can fix it or make it any better.

No more. Today's the day it ends. After three years, the time has come to put the thing to rest. I flick my cigarette away and head inside, to finish my shift and make plans for later.

* * *

When work is through, I fill a cup of espresso dregs and take it with me. Down on Main Street, I stop by the local florist and buy a red rose and then drive along the route called Old Sutter Road. Before stepping out of my car onto the sun-baked cemetery parking lot, I ask myself what the point is. But I know the answer all too well: because there's a thing haunting my life and it will never, ever go away until I finally confront it.

The quarter-mile walk to the plot is a winding, deserted path of silent grass and static trees, all hedged in by a gaudy chain-link fence. Heat bears down like a crack to hell has opened up above me. I find the proper row, skip a few graves over, and I'm there.

There's a thing in my mother's coffin. It scratches at the inside of the lid, shouting curses reduced to babble by the six feet of dirt above it. Nevertheless, the emotions it expresses are clear, stuff I've heard so many times I know it all by rote. Utter disappointment. Hate. But mostly regret for the life and freedom ruined by my unexpected birth.

She killed herself three years ago. She should be dead and gone and yet she returns as the thing in all my things, a malignant voice manifesting the poisonous words she fed me all my life. But now I'll say my own words, kept locked away because of fear, because of deep-seated self-contempt. Because it hurts too much to voice aloud, no matter how true they are.

"For thirty years, you were a terrible mother. A monster, a hateful, selfish thing. I never said it before because I loved you, but I can't let you hurt me anymore. You're dead and buried and that's all you're allowed to be."

I lay the flower on her plot, a symbol of my enduring love. As for the rest of me, the greater part? I dump the cup of espresso dregs, as bitter and cold as was her constant disposition. It drips down her tombstone, trickling across the words, "Loving Mother, Died Too Soon," etched into its face. Then I spit on the grass above the remains of what has always been her small, decaying heart.

* * *

There's a thing in my head, inhabiting the darkest grooves and wrinkles of my brain. It tells me terrible, degrading lies—lies that poke and prod and tear and hurt—and sometimes I still believe them. But now, for the first time since my mother's death, my memories are the only place it haunts.

MULTO

M Y FATHER LIKED TO SAY, "*Ang nakaraan ay hindi kailanman nawawala, nalilimutan lamang,*" or rather, "The past is never gone, only forgotten." Whether a *salawikain* of the Philippines or something he made up, it seemed to fit, and I'd come across no better example than when I received an unexpected friend request online. It came with a message: *Adan, can we talk? There's something you need to know,* and then, *Remember the multo?*

The profile included a blurry photo of a forty-something Filipina woman by the name of Dakila Hayes. Her hair black, straight, and shoulder length, and lips drawn up in a not-quite-there smile. Though she had a new last name, new creases near her eyes, and a hardening of her jawline, I could never forget that face.

"That's strange," I said, swiveling my computer chair around.

My wife Jana lay slumped against the armrest of the couch, a blanket wrapped around her legs. Some documentary about the BTK Killer streamed on Netflix, but she had her attention fixed solely on her phone—the way she always "watched" TV.

"What?" she asked.

"A neighbor from...God, maybe thirty years ago, contacted me out of the blue."

"What'd they want?"

"She asked me if I remembered the '*multo,*'" I said, using finger quotes. "In Tagalog, that means ghost."

Jana laughed, wrinkled her nose. "Well, now I'm curious. Do you?"

My forehead creased as I pored through distant memories. Above the rest, a single name fought to the forefront of my mind, and with it a scattershot of images and emotions I hadn't thought about or felt in years. "Actually, I think I do. We called it the Black Thing."

* * *

When I was six, my family moved from an apartment into the bottom floor of a two-story duplex in Oakland, California. My parents had scrimped for years before they collected enough money for the down payment on that place. As migrants from the Philippines, it became the first piece of US property they owned, and they were proud of it. Despite its sunken ceilings and dripping copper-colored stains. Despite its thin, bowing walls, and floorboards that pitched up in places, begging to put splinters big as toothpicks in our feet. Despite the boys of *Norteños*, who took over the neighborhood by sundown, and kept my parents up some nights with shouts and screams, and the occasional burst of gunfire.

They instituted strict rules to keep me and my siblings safe, though gangs, and drugs, and violence didn't worry me back then. My own fear came the day the Jacobes moved into the upper floor of our duplex. Being the only Filipino families on the street, our parents became instant friends, the sort of bond that could only exist when natural-born Pinoy met so far from the homeland. At least once a week, we all came together to eat Filipino cuisine: *lumpia*, chicken *adobo*, *daing*, maybe even *balut*—because who the hell else wouldn't judge us when the egg shell broke, revealing a duck or chicken fetus spilling from its own juices?

When the adults passed out the halo-halo, they convened in the living room and made us children go outside. Since Dakila and Arnel Jacobe were much older than us, we never played. Usually, they took me, Tala, and Amado to the front stoop where we talked, and sometimes shared scary stories of ghosts and demons that haunted the Philippines. They told us about Balete Drive in a place called Quezon City, where spirits inhabit the trees, or walk the dusty corridors of old mansions, and the apparition of a White Lady stalks the street at night. They told us about the city of San Juan, where the head of the Stabbed Priest searches for his body, the

Headless Nun sneaks up on unsuspecting passersby, and the Devil Cigar Man drags victims to hell if they don't offer him a light. They even told us about a special *multo*, the one that followed the Jacobes across the ocean, from city to city and house to house.

"Usually, *mga multo* remain in the places where they died," said Dakila. "But sometimes they grow attached to a person and stay with them until the end. This one is attached to our grandma. She says it's different from all the others, darker, an evil thing."

"It said it was coming for her," said Arnel. "It said that her soul was his to take, and that her flesh and bones were his to feast upon once her body was an empty shell."

Until then, I'd lived a sheltered life of cartoons and children's books, where getting chased by wasps or falling into a river of chocolate were the worst things that could happen. The idea of tormenting ghosts terrified me like nothing else. I didn't want to believe it, but the conviction on their faces made it hard for me to doubt.

"Really?" I said, wide-eyed and breathless.

"Of course. Grandma never lies," said Arnel.

"Never, never," said Dakila.

* * *

I'd always accepted the fact that life entailed growing old, changing in increments so small they could never be quantified. And so, confronted by this token of the past, the string of subtle changes I'd undergone the last thirty years stood out like a glaring metamorphosis. Though I could feel a hint of the boy I was, he had become a stranger to me.

My own children had turned six and eight this year. I wondered about the things that kept them up at night, and whether they faced the same worries and concerns that I had, or if this new generation had new burdens that I would never understand. As I passed their doors, I had the sudden urge to peek inside and see how they were doing. In the first room, Peter lay on his bed reading one of my old *Groo* comics, his crusty shoes pressed into his bedspread.

"Are you doing okay?" I asked.

"Yep."

"Good. Then take off your sneakers; you know better."

"Yep," he said, and kicked both shoes to the floor.

In the next room, Stacy crouched beside her dollhouse, asking questions of her dolls, and then supplying answers in a high-pitched squeak. She didn't muster so much as a glance in my direction, but I didn't need her to confirm what I could already see. She was okay too.

While heading to my own room, I wondered at this sudden concern for their well-being. I thought about it the entire time I stripped and dressed in worn-out clothes more suitable for yard work. The answer that came up could be summarized in one word: fear. As a husband and a father, intangible horrors—like *mga multo*—were meaningless to me now, but my parents' fear of the *Norteños*, and the chance their children might suffer from some random violent act? That I understood.

Still, one of the *salawikain* my father taught me lingered in my mind like a warning: "*Ang gawa sa pagkabata dala hanggang pagtanda.*" ("What one learns in childhood he carries into adulthood.") And I wondered how and when that truth would play itself out.

* * *

My house in Oklahoma City was more spacious and preserved than the Oakland duplex, but they had a few minor traits in common. Both were two-story relics built sometime in the 1930s, with wiring that couldn't always keep up with a modern family's needs. Both had the tendency to speak their minds at night, through the groans of pipes, random thumps, or the creaks of settling wood. They both also had a place of idling darkness.

Here, it was the garage. The sun had almost set when I stepped through the garage's back door entrance, the smell of dust and thick, moist air settling around me. It weighed heavy on my lungs and made the room feel somehow smaller, like the back of a long cavern, or the inside of a crypt. I slid my hand along the studs of the unfinished walls and flipped the light switch. The single bulb dangling from the ceiling swayed from a breeze blowing through the open door, yet the deepest shadows held their place. They shifted from muddled splotches to tenebrous shapes, a thousand undulating faces all staring at me.

In that moment, I could hear the bell toll, warning of the Headless Nun. Could hear the raucous laughter of the Devil Cigar Man, the White Lady sighing in my ear, the distant cries of the

Stabbed Priest. Mere whispers. A figment of my imagination. And yet I couldn't stop the goosebumps rising on my arms, or the tickle at the nape of my neck that made the hairs there stand on end.

Once the feeling ran its course, I grabbed my mower and left far quicker than I'd care to admit. It was funny. I'd gone into the garage a thousand times before, but never experienced the slightest bit of discomfort. It was as if Dakila's friend request had stirred up more than memories, had in fact awakened a part of me from long ago—a part that shivered when the lights went off because it still believed in the inherent truths of childhood. Like sometimes we have a right to be afraid. Because sometimes the darkness isn't empty.

* * *

Dakila and Arnel's grandmother only spoke Tagalog. Whenever we visited the Jacobes, she would fix us with a hard stare and shout, "Maiingay na mga bata!" ("Noisy children!"), before hobbling back to the privacy of her room. Some nights, through the floorboards, we'd hear her screams, and the muffled voices of her family trying to placate her. She was such a strange character, the perfect blend of mysterious and creepy, that she made Dakila and Arnel's stories feel more real. As such, when the details surrounding her harassing multo increased, so did our fascination with the subject.

My siblings and I dubbed it the Black Thing. We spent a lot of time giving substance and meaning to its existence, beyond what we had heard. If someone escaped our notice for a few days, we would say the Black Thing held them prisoner. If something of ours went missing, we would say the Black Thing stole it. And when someone stripped the lock in our front door, shattered my mother's favorite ceramic pot, and cracked a slat in our fence, we said the Black Thing was in a rage.

Though it had evolved into a shared creation, I may have been the only one in my family who actually believed in it, and as the youngest by at least three years, my siblings teased me without mercy. Especially when it came to the Black Thing's so-called lair. Since the duplex had been built upon a hillside, it lengthened at its rear to match the sloping ground, exposing the south side of the basement. Neither the Jacobes nor our parents ever went inside, save to check the fuse box or the water heater. As such, it remained largely untouched, its insides tinted gray from layered dust, and infested by bugs and vermin. The windows reflected sunlight in the day and absorbed darkness at night so that it had the habit of resisting peering eyes. Taken altogether, it acted as the perfect focus for our macabre imaginings. The place of idling dark in my childhood years.

Whenever we played in our back yard, my brother and sister never failed to steal a glance in its direction.

"Did you see that?" said Tala, eyes wide, mouth gaping. "Through the window. I think I saw eyes."

"Yeah, I saw it too," said Amado. "Something's watching us right now. Something big. Something hungry."

"Quit it, guys," I said.

"We're serious," said Tala.

Amado gestured at the house. "I think we should tell Mom and Dad."

"No, you know how Dad is. He'd only try to investigate and end up getting hurt. Or worse, killed."

A subtle tremble in my chest spread to my limbs. I imagined movement, some dark shape crawling just beneath the window sills, its fingers gnarled, and claws as big as knives. My face flushed warm and I fought the sudden urge to run and hide, my aversion to my siblings' disapproval only slightly greater than my fear of death. "Come on, guys, stop kidding around."

"This is no joke," said Amado.

"Do we even look like we're kidding?" asked Tala.

Not then, of course. I mistook their lively performance and solemn expressions as honest-to-God truth, and I paid the price for it with many lonely, sleepless nights.

*   *   *

Night fell quicker than I could finish my yard work, and I spent the last five minutes mowing in the gloom of dusk. As shadows pooled over the wide stretch of my back yard, my imagination soared with eerie thoughts. Whispers hid within the rustling of branches. Somewhere in the distance, I heard a scream or what might have been a stray cat's caterwaul. Glints of light reflected from behind the shrub across the yard, or was it eyes peering from the cover of the foliage?

I gathered my things in a hurry, dragged the mower to the back door of the garage, but hesitated when I noticed the lights were off.

I told myself it didn't matter. I wasn't a child, or a coward, and had long ago outgrown the silly fear of ghosts and monsters. Nevertheless, my hand refused to probe the darkness, and my legs refused to take a step inside. Instead, I shoved the mower, let it roll, let it drift back to its proper place, and fled into the house.

Jana, seated at the computer desk, turned when the door creaked shut behind me. She must have sensed my mood because she asked, "What's wrong?"

"Nothing," I said. "Just tired, is all."

"I was about to call you in. It's the kids' bedtime, and your turn to read them a story tonight." She headed for the staircase, but halted on the second step. "I almost forgot. You got a PM, but I didn't recognize the name. Maybe that old neighbor you mentioned?"

"All right. I'll be up in a second."

I dropped to the computer chair and logged into my account, though I wasn't eager to read Dakila's new message. Nothing good could come of it. Enough had already bubbled up from the cracks of my subconscious for me to know I was better off forgetting, and I worried what else might slip through before the day was finished.

Dakila's message read: *Kumusta ka? How is your family? I live twenty miles from that old duplex where my parents still live. They sometimes ask about your parents and wonder how they're doing.* And then she got to the crux: *The reason I contacted you is because my grandma passed away. Her funeral was last week.*

I wrote: *Kumusta kayo? I'm sorry to hear about your grandmother. She seemed like a good woman who lived a long life. She will be missed.*

I was about to shut the computer down when a new message appeared on my screen.

Do you remember the multo *Arnel and I used to tell you about?* Dakila wrote.

Yes, I wrote.

And do you remember the story you told us about that multo, *shortly before you moved away?*

I did. Of course I did. No matter how deep I had tried to bury it in layers of avoidance and distractions, it didn't take much for it to extract itself from beneath the decades of lost memories. For a moment, I thought back to a particular day from those early Oakland years, one I'd desperately hoped I would never have to think about again.

* * *

Sometimes Tala, Amado, and I would pretend we were superheroes, and we always played rough. Once we chose our favorite characters from a few, old, battered copies of *Justice League*, we'd jump and bounce and thrash around on our bunk bed without a thought for our own safety. One night, I shot a hand out to block an invisible villain's punch, and my elbow smashed into the brittle sheetrock beside the bottom bunk. A hole opened into the house's skeletal frame. We could only stare at the damage, frozen by a mutual fear of grounding, and all too aware of the cool, stale air pouring through.

When my parents heard the noise, they rushed into our room. They didn't yell at us like we expected, but they made their irritation clear.

"It is late. I am too tired to fix it right now," my father said.

"But it's cold," said Amado.

"And it smells weird," said Tala.

"You should have thought about that before you acted rashly. Maybe now you will be more careful," my mother said.

Bedtime came, and the three of us crawled under our covers: Tala on the top bunk, and Amado and me on the bottom, facing opposite directions. Since I had made the hole, Amado made me sleep in front of it. Our parents shut the lights, said their goodnights, and closed the door.

Though the darkness was complete, I stared in the direction of the hole, convinced holding it within my line of sight would keep me safe—or at least forewarned. Even though I tried to forget, my mind picked through details of every *multo* story I could remember, and I shivered. Not from the cold draft the hole allowed, but because of what it meant. "The Black Thing sleeps below us," Dakila had once said, and now there was a passageway that spanned the distance from its lair into our room.

Before long, Tala began to snore, and Amado's deep, full breaths meant he too had fallen asleep. Every quiet noise amplified into a raucous sound, second only to the staccato beating of my heart. Something by the dresser thumped. Beyond the ceiling, groans erupted in a random pattern that defied the path of any normal pipeline. A brief silence, and then a rush of air like an exhale or a sigh spilled into my ear. I looked around, tried to latch on to the sight of something real, something solid, but everything was lost within the squirming dark.

A faint scratching skittered up from somewhere down below. I pictured the Black Thing climbing through the space inside the walls, mirroring the sound as it grew closer. Once the scratching crossed into my room, I pulled the covers over my head, and nudged my brother with my foot. He didn't move. I whispered, "Amado," but he didn't answer. I kicked him hard enough to jar him, but he only grunted, shifted to his side, and fell still. Hot tears slid down my face. I listened for my parents' footsteps, hoping that any second they would open the door, turn on the lights, and sweep this nightmare away for good. I begged for it, prayed, but no one came.

The smell of dust, and sweat, and moldering fabric wafted in. A need to scream swelled heavy in my chest, but I locked my throat, choked it down. If the Black Thing heard me now, it would know I was awake, but if I kept still and quiet, maybe I'd be safe. Invisible.

A soft, taunting laugh crept in, too close to mistake its source. Then a voice, deep but whispered, said, "*Nakikita kita.*" ("I see you.")

This time I didn't stop my scream, but nothing louder than a breath escaped my mouth. My body begged me to get up and run, but I was far too scared for that. The presence loomed above me, its face inches from my own, and I imagined its cold stare piercing the thin fabric of the blanket that separated us. Hands draped across my chest. They slowly pressed down, my ribs aching as it squeezed the air out of my lungs, the chill of its skin absorbing my warmth.

"When the old woman dies, you and I will meet again," it said. "*Sa ibang araw.*"

Its last words trailed like a dying echo, and with it the Black Thing faded too. After a time—I couldn't say how long—my voice returned, and I screamed over and over, louder and louder, until the bedroom door burst open, and light flooded my room.

"What is it? What is wrong?" my father said, rushing to my bedside.

I tore the covers off, threw myself from bed, mashed my face against his legs and hugged him close. I stared into the hole—now empty save for dust and cobwebs—and then turned to my brother and sister now sitting up in bed. Their bleary eyes and stark confusion told me everything I needed. They hadn't seen or heard a thing. I had been alone, and that realization left me dazed and silent for the rest of the night.

* * *

I slouched in front of my computer screen, trying to compose myself. Those memories had lain dormant for so long I didn't know how to take them. While I knew they couldn't possibly be true, the feelings they invoked and the fears they uncovered were all too real.

Wow, I wrote. *Can't believe you remember that. I'm embarrassed. I had a strong imagination as a kid, that's for sure.*

So, everything is okay? she asked. *You're safe?*

Of course. Why shouldn't I be?

You of all people should know how difficult it is for me to share this, but I need you to understand. My grandma was never the same after the multo *attached to her. She grew increasingly distant from the rest of us, disconnected from reality, tormented by things only she could hear and see.*

I don't understand. Why are you telling me this?

Because of what it told you. Remember? Sa ibang araw.

Someday.

Exactly.

* * *

I thanked Dakila for her concern, insisted I was fine. We made plans to catch up later, and then I joined Jana and the kids upstairs. We started a new book—Roald Dahl's *The Twits*, a childhood favorite— and the good memories and my children's laughter helped to calm me, if only a little.

Not long after, Jana and I went to sleep as well. While lying in bed together, I tried to tell her about what Dakila had said, and everything I'd remembered. I couldn't. I told myself I didn't need to concern her with superstitious nonsense, but the greater part of me knew that was a lie. I was afraid, and to admit that to myself would mean embracing the truth that the *multo* was real, that it was out there, searching for me. And if it ever found me, our lives would never be the same.

Jana cut the lights, and within minutes I heard her winsome snores. As for me, I couldn't sleep, didn't dare shut my eyes for fear of what I might see when I opened them again. A deeper darkness spread throughout our room, blotting everything around me. Soon, like so many nights before, the house spoke its mind. The pipes beyond the ceiling groaned. Heavy footsteps passed through the garage beneath us. A shuffle in the living room, and then slow, deliberate creaks ascended the stairs, stopping only when they'd reached the landing outside our bedroom door.

My breath caught, and I felt the sudden urge to cover my face with blankets. Was it settling wood this time? Or had "someday" finally come?

HOLLOW SKULLS

W*E'VE FINALLY MADE A family, and nothing can go wrong.*

* * *

Orson took the long way home from the hospital, along gravel back roads that cut through miles of empty fields and scattered stands of birches. It added an extra thirty minutes to their drive, but his wife Martha insisted it would be safer that way.

"Precious cargo," she said from the back seat, caressing their newborn Gabriel's face with her finger.

At the sight of their proximity, Orson's cheeks flushed. He wiped fresh sweat pooling on his forehead and nodded at her reflection in the rearview mirror. Not in agreement, just to acknowledge she'd spoken.

When he pulled up to their house, Martha was the first one out. By the time he unbuckled the baby seat, she'd rounded the car, her slumped gait painting red and pink spider-web splotches across her face.

"Martha—"

She put a finger to his lips. "I know what you're going to say, but I want to be the one to carry him inside."

He shook his head. "The doctor said—"

"Oh, who cares what that old quack thinks!"

She crossed her arms and grinned, the middle of her cheeks sinking into dimples. Despite an avalanche of fears, he couldn't bring himself to say no to that face.

Martha lifted Gabriel from his chair and held him snug in her arms, as if he were slick and fragile, squirming to get loose, and not merely sleeping. Orson wrapped an arm around her and led them both inside. Once they reached the nursery, he hesitated, averting his eyes from the newly painted walls. Even with the many coats of blue he'd laid down last week, a shade of pink still bled through the surface, vague but somehow blinding.

Martha shuffled to the crib and set Gabriel down. "Orson, come say hi to our son," she said, waving him farther in.

He tottered to her side and held her close, absorbing the warmth, the feel, and smell of her.

"What do you think?" said Martha.

The pristine white of the crib and blankets surrounding Gabriel made Orson feel somehow safer, as if the purity implied would leach out all the darkness, leaving his son's insides clean and gleaming. He imagined Gabriel with angel wings, and for a moment he let himself believe it.

We've finally made a family, and nothing can go wrong.

"He's...beautiful," Orson said, but the illusion of innocence vanished. In his mind, the angel wings shriveled into gashes and a nub of horns broke through the thin brown skin of Gabriel's forehead.

Martha must have noticed the change in Orson's demeanor because she pressed her lips into a perfect line and said, "Oh, Orson. I know you're afraid. I am too, but whatever happened with Michelle can't possibly..." She shook her head, glanced at the walls and quickly turned away. "This time things will be different."

"Yes. I'll make sure of that," he said. "I promise."

* * *

Martha turned in at sundown. Though she'd stayed a few extra days in the hospital, the strain of a thirty-hour delivery had taken a severe toll on her already weakened body. She fell asleep as soon as Orson tucked the sheets under her chin, her lungs whooping heavy with every breath.

Orson lay in bed beside her, watching her, envying the easy

way she rested, the way her smile followed her even into sleep. Such peace seemed beyond him now, fixed to a time and place so far gone he could hardly remember it. He cupped her cheek, whispered comfort and kind words, and once he was sure she wouldn't wake, he slipped into the hallway.

The air felt thick and cramped, as if there weren't enough space for the pieces of him to fit. The refrigerator hummed and gurgled in the kitchen and Orson's footsteps thumped to its rhythm. He peered inside the doorway of the nursery. The only illumination came from a nightlight, ethereal streaks of primary colors cast by a plastic butterfly cover. After matching dark shapes up to memories, and seeing nothing out of place, he gathered his courage and edged up to the crib.

Even in the dim light he could make out the details of Gabriel's face: eyes closed, mouth shifting between a smile and a grimace, body jerking back and forth from some unknown dreamtime impulse. A baby in repose? Or was it something worse?

Orson's grandmother had a different name for newborns: not he or she, but "it" or "vessel." Hollow skulls, waiting like an empty truck cab with the engine left running. Whenever she got going, and the fire in her gut warmed over, she would let loose a litany about it—the same way a backwoods yokel might rant about Bigfoot.

"Most of the time, the cab remains without a driver and the vessel's allowed to age enough so that the soul blooms in the soft soil of its mind. But sometimes? Sometimes *they* come first," Orson's grandmother had said.

He was barely ten at the time, and while he wasn't sure his grandmother's words were gospel truth, they still scratched the itch of curiosity.

"Who do you mean? Who are *they?*" Orson asked.

She'd played the question in her mind, in a way that made her eyebrows dance. Then she'd said, "The old gods who ruled the chaos before creation. Or monsters made before the world began. Who can say for sure? All I know is what they do, and what they do is desecrate the innocent."

Those last words haunted Orson even now, playing havoc with his senses. Shadows darted at him from across the nursery floor, forcing him back into the hallway. Hidden behind the gurgle of the fridge, he heard hushed and ruffled laughter. With that, he slunk back to his bedroom, wondering one last thing: how many days or months until he could get some peace of mind, until he knew for sure whether he should celebrate or mourn for the coming of his son.

* * *

Heavy rainfall dulled the morning sky, but by early afternoon the sunlight burst through cloud cover and warmed over a new spring day. Martha decided it was the perfect time to take Gabriel to the park.

"No. You need your rest," Orson said, but Martha wouldn't hear it.

"I've rested enough. Besides, some fresh air will do us all some good."

Martha clutched Orson's arm while he pushed the stroller. The sight and sound of birds chirping among the blossoms on trees left her warm and smiling, gazing all around. But Orson kept his focus on the baby. Gabriel seemed a little too interested in the things around him for a week-old someone who only saw in blurs. Or was it new smells and the steady drone of sounds he'd never heard before? Either way, Orson made a mental note of it and stowed it away for later.

The neighborhood was arrayed in its usual weekend bustle. Across the street a crowd gathered at a yard sale. Other neighbors watered or mowed their lawns, or weeded and pruned their gardens. No one took the slightest interest in Orson and his family, except Mrs. Rhodes, an elderly widow who lived at the end of the block. As she approached the passing family from her porch, she joined her hands together and aimed her grin beneath the shade of the stroller's hood.

"Oh, what a little angel," she said.

"Isn't he?" said Martha.

As if on cue, Gabriel puckered his lips and a milky string dribbled down his chin. Mrs. Rhodes and Martha tilted their heads and blurted, "Awww," but Orson merely grimaced. Somewhere in the false calm of his mind, he could hear his grandmother's voice, huffing and scoffing in turns. She was a different breed, that woman. If Martha and Mrs. Rhodes were cut from the same dreamy spool of silk, she was hacksawed from a rusted sheet of metal.

Orson thought back to the time when she sat him down before his cousin's christening. He was twelve then, dressed in a black suit and tie, staring at his reflection in his newly polished shoes with no small amount of pride. While all the other members of their family were still getting dressed, she took him into the living room and sat him on the sofa. She kneeled before him, looked into his eyes, urging her face forward as if to give her words a prod.

"Make no mistake; some vessels are pretty things through and through. But sometimes you'll see one and you'll know that it's gone wrong. Keep a sharp eye out and see if you can't spot it for yourself. Their skin splotched red and pink, like flesh too scrubbed by scouring pads. Their hair stuck out like thin wires, cheeks bulging round as infected plums. Eyelids held in slits so that only the deep, deep dark of their pupils lay exposed."

"Is that what Aunt Tabby's baby looks like?" Orson had asked.

"I don't know yet," she'd said. "What I do know is the uglier it is, the closer they've come. Touched it somehow, put their mark upon its skin."

Mrs. Rhodes took her leave, and Orson and Martha carried on a few more blocks into the park. The benches were full of chattering parents, a kid planted on every swing and a line at every slide. Martha seemed delighted by the sight of them. She moved closer to Orson's ear and said, "Soon he'll be that old too. They grow up so fast."

How he wanted it to be true. He pictured Gabriel a four-foot strapping boy, one of the many gamboling children punching footprints in the sand. A normal child, untainted by what his grandmother had long warned him of. Hope surged within him and he sneaked a glance in his son's direction.

We've finally made a family, and nothing can go wrong.

Gabriel stared back, the black of his thin-slit eyes an endless sea of nothing, the red lines of his exposed skin like deep-etched omens. Two sure signs as plain as day.

* * *

Gabriel's cries swelled heavy in the narrow walls of the hallway. Martha heard sadness, but Orson could almost taste their baby's true intent. There were curses flitting among each forlorn shriek, babble uttered in an unholy language. He wanted to plug his ears to it, to pretend it'd gone away, but Martha wouldn't let him.

"We already fed and changed him," Orson said. "He's fine. Babies need to scream, that's all."

"I can't help feeling like there's something wrong," Martha said. "What if he hurt himself? Or what if someone's in his room and they try to take him away, like they took our—"

"Shhh, sweetie. I'll go and check if you promise me you'll rest," he said, before the idea took root, and the lie he'd fed her about their daughter Michelle came spilling from her lips.

Orson crept down the hallway, deeper into the black throat of the monster's lair. He was conscious of the walls and a feeling like something, or *things*, watched him from the dark corners and the shadows, measuring the way he moved, his every step. The pipes in the ceiling knocked, smothering the sound of almost-voices uttered just below a whisper. When he entered the nursery, Gabriel began thrashing in his crib, his face crimson, his eyelids mashed into thick black lines and his mouth a toothless oval.

"Settle down. It's me. I know what you really are, so there's no use wasting all that energy."

He said it as a test, to see how Gabriel would react. But if Gabriel understood, he gave no hint and the guessing game continued—along with all the crying.

Despite a slick and cold sensation worming across Orson's skin, he scooped up Gabriel in his arms and rocked him. He began to sing a lullaby, one Martha taught him shortly after Michelle was born. Alongside it, a thought lumbered through his mind of a night much like this one, in this very room. It shook the dust off memories he'd long since left behind and put a lump too thick to swallow in his throat.

"There was a time when I believed you had one," his grandmother had said as he cradled and shushed Michelle.

"Really?" asked Orson. "Why?"

"This was after your father left and you and your mother came to live with me. You were empty still, barely a month, and the nights were long and dappled by your ungodly screeches."

"Oh, Grandma. Babies cry. That's what they do,"

"One that's clean? Well fed? Comfortable?" she said, inching her round and disbelieving face closer to his.

"Yes, even them."

"Yeah right. The doctors named it colic, as if pinning a word on the unexplained somehow makes it better. But I know the truth. No healthy body ever needs to scream in pain."

"So what are you saying? Did I have one or not?"

"No, thank our lucky stars. Turned out to be a fractured bone is all. The question is, does *it* have a fractured bone as well?"

They had stared at Michelle while she kept on thrashing. From the very start, she was terrified when Orson's grandmother was around. Not even the presence of Orson offered any solace as she cracked sobs through the wide gulf of her mouth, almost begging for release.

And now, so did Gabriel.

* * *

Orson had violent dreams. In them, Gabriel seized Martha's breast and began to suck the life from her. Orson was forced to watch from behind a glass wall he couldn't move or break as her body turned cadaverous and then fell into a heap of empty flesh. He woke up gasping for air and threw a glance at Martha. She lay limp and unconscious, chest sunken as if crumpled by the weight of her exhaustion. He gave her a quick kiss on the cheek and quietly left the room.

The polite stutter of her snores trailed him to the nursery where he watched Gabriel at rest. Martha's pregnancy had been hard. Nine months of headaches and vomiting while the soft globe of her belly slowly inflated to a boulder. Constant bleeds led right up to Gabriel's birth, spotting Martha's clothes and bed sheets with black dollops and red spots. Even then, he'd found it hard to believe her condition wasn't a sign of things to come: the little leech hurting her insides for the pure sake of cruelty.

That was when the nightmares had begun. Some variation of her murder and the funeral that followed, where a closed casket hid the mess of what his then-future child had left behind. It tired him to no end. Aged him, drawing lines of worry on his face so that, by the time the slog through pregnancy had ended, he looked more like a grandfather than a father. But Martha, through ignorance, had held onto her youthful vigor, and he loved her all the more because of it. He would let that ignorance persist as long as he could. And in the meantime? He'd just have to keep the two apart.

He made breakfast. By the time the eggs hardened and the hash browns caked, an undulating *creak* sounded from the living room. He looked through the kitchen door at Martha seated on the couch, her shirt pulled up and left breast mashed between Gabriel's anxious lips.

Orson fought against the wild panic that drove the strength out from his knees. He wanted to yell at her for the danger she'd put herself in, but a stream of violent images filled his mind: Gabriel's teeth sinking into Martha's carotid artery; Gabriel seated by her still, dead body, bathing in a pool of her blood; Gabriel carving crosshatch marks into her skin while laughing, always laughing.

Clinging to the countertop was all he could do to keep himself from falling down. It proved more than he could bear and he found his hand crawling spider-like across the countertop, to the knife block, where his fingers curled around the synthetic handle of the chef's knife.

"I didn't want to wake you," he said, barely comprehending his own words above mere chatter.

"I heard Gabriel crying. Poor little thing. I think he missed his mommy. And her milk."

The ferocity with which Gabriel drank hypnotized Orson; all that wet slurping and lip smacking, like a predatory animal devouring its prey. He couldn't shut out the idea that Gabriel was just feigning impotence, to amplify the moment he attacked, and he shuddered even as Martha hissed in pain.

"What? What's wrong? Are you hurt?" he shouted, pulling the knife free, holding it tight and ready at his side.

Martha grinned, cheeks dimpled. "He pinched me."

"I thought..." He shook his head. "Never mind," he said, letting the tension ease away from the muscles in his arms and shoulders.

"What were you going to do with that?" said Martha, nodding to the knife.

He shot it a glance and his eyes went wide with knowing. "Nothing. I don't know. I wanted to, maybe, cut some ham for breakfast."

"I don't think we have any left," said Martha.

"No, you're right. I didn't find any either," he said, and slipped the knife back in the block.

* * *

Another night, and they convened in the living room. Martha spoke over the blare of evening news, gushing plans for Gabriel's future: shopping trips to buy him clothes, visits out of state to show him off to family, and even what private school he should attend.

"And I want Pastor Labberton to perform Gabriel's baptism. He has a good heart, that man. Michelle seemed so happy when he held her. Do you remember?"

He nodded. Of course he did. He remembered the jealousy he felt seeing her eyes alight and the small upward creases at the corners of her mouth when she passed into the pastor's care. Only hindsight had revealed the truth: that Michelle had already been taken over and her so-called smile was nothing more than the smug elation of an ancient thing, gloating over the corruption of his daughter.

Orson thought about how Gabriel would react to his own baptism and whether it would be much the same as Michelle's. He found himself staring at his son lying in the baby chair, a plastic set of keys and a truck dangling from a bar above his face. The irony of that empty truck cab wasn't lost on Orson—and neither was Gabriel's behavior.

Every so often, Orson caught a glimpse of Gabriel's eyelids dragging open, watching them with a face full of knowing. But the moment Gabriel noticed he was being watched, his eyes snapped shut and he gave a gurgled sigh, as if he'd just eased into a peaceful rest. A small part of Orson still wanted to believe it was true, no matter how sad and wearying the act of hoping had become.

We've finally made a family and nothing can go wrong.

But the voice of his grandmother broke through his optimistic shell, reminding him of lessons he had learned, decisions he had made, and the repercussions that—even after all these years—still festered like an open wound inside him.

"You've seen the signs. There's no mistake," his grandmother had said.

"I can't," Orson had said, pacing the living room of his house, pressing fists against his cheeks to smear his tears. "Not my—"

"Vessel?"

"Daughter!" he shouted, near snarling.

"Don't be fooled, Orson. That's what *they* want you to think, but you know better."

He charged at his grandmother and leaned in close, spitting rage into her face. "Are you even listening to what you're saying? You're crazy! She's just a baby!"

"Because it's from your loins? Because it bears a likeness to you and Martha, it can't be something evil? If it had slithered from the shadows of your closet, you would have called it monster. If it had dug its way out from the cold, dead earth, you would have called it demon. But no, its darkness was the womb, its portal the birth canal, and so you call it, simply, baby."

Michelle screamed in the nursery and he heard it as a cry of torment. Michelle had never once felt anything like safe in his arms, but he had to try to comfort her. Despite what his grandmother believed had grown inside her, she was still his daughter, his baby girl.

His grandmother placed a hand against his chest.

"Get out of my way," he said.

She tensed, a frown wrinkling her face like the crevices of a sandstone hillside. "Think, Orson! There's more at stake than that vessel's life."

"I've had enough of this, enough of your stories, enough of your bullshit! Get out of my—"

"Daddy?"

Orson and his grandmother turned to face the throbbing darkness of the hallway.

"Daddy, where are you? I'm scared. I need you."

The voice was a candy-coated thing, the high-pitched sound of helium seeping out of virgin lungs. Orson had imagined Michelle would sound that way someday, when she'd grown, matured, and added at least a half a decade more to the fragment of her life. But not now. Not at a month. He stared at his grandmother, his face empty of emotions save the tears of anguish clouding his eyes.

"I'll go," she said, patting his shoulder. "I can see this is too much for you. Let the burden fall on me."

He nodded and closed his eyes, thought about Martha. They'd sent her off, unaware, on a weekend getaway with her friends at a local spa resort. She left as a mother and a loving wife, but what would she be upon her return? He couldn't even fathom, didn't want to. Almost as an afterthought, he said, "Grandma. Try to save her. Please."

His grandmother had scowled, made as if to speak, but shook her head. "If I can, I will."

Martha's voice lifted Orson out from all those tainted memories and he took in a great big burst of air as if he'd been holding his breath.

"That's it? Finished already, little guy?" she asked.

Gabriel grunted as he loosened from her nipple. He'd had his fill for now, but how much longer until that milk no longer satisfied, and the empty space inside him filled with the same evil that took Michelle? Orson wouldn't allow it. He couldn't let that happen. For

Martha's sake, he had to act before it was too late.

* * *

Martha succumbed to sleep the moment she laid her head down on her pillow. Orson lay in bed beside her, bursting with nervous energy that made his stomach churn and his body shake. He whispered prayers inside his head—*Let me be right. Dear God in Heaven, don't let me do this unless I'm right*—while he waited. Two grueling hours passed, slow as lifetimes, before he could convince himself it was safe enough to rise.

He went first into the kitchen to retrieve the weapon he'd prepared. Experience had taught him a simple blade of steel could kill them; one solid blow through the heart or brain to sever all connections. He chose the chef's knife from before. It had a good heft and the edge was razor sharp, something he'd maintained ever since Michelle's death.

He entered the nursery next. This time no pipes knocked, the multicolored nightlight cover cast a bland and basic light, and even the darkness remained inert, not living things but shadows. Gabriel lay inside the crib, docile on his blankets, his lips forming a kiss. Orson crushed the handle of the knife in both hands.

"I have to," he said, short of a whisper, too low to the let the world, or even his own ears, judge the worth of it.

He raised the knife high, tasting blood from the part of his cheek caught between his teeth, and then... He let his arms slacken at his sides. In that meager light, Gabriel could have been statue or a doll for all the innocence he exuded. He could have even been a newborn baby, a son. There was nothing ruthless in Orson now, so he went back to those memories of Michelle's last night.

His grandmother had left him in the living room alone. A quiet enfolded him, magnifying the gentle bumps and scuffles from the nursery. There came a bestial shriek, a squeal of pure madness, and a sound like boards being torn up from the flooring echoed through the house. The noise prickled against his skin and ears and his heart throbbed in sympathetic agony.

"No, wait!" he yelled, scrambling for the nursery as if fire were licking at his heels.

He meant to stop his grandmother from doing Michelle any more harm, hoping there was still a chance to save his daughter. But when he entered the nursery, he dropped to his knees, staring in disbelief. The world shattered into tiny fragments, save for one diminutive form, one revolting silhouette stitched together from every repellent thing of a parent's greatest nightmares: his Michelle, his baby daughter, twisted, corrupted—by that thing inhabiting her body—into a mockery of infanthood.

Beneath Michelle lay his grandmother with her neck snapped, her clothes torn, arms and legs bent in all the wrong directions. In a flurry of confusion and fear, he snatched up his grandmother's knife and threw himself at Michelle. She toppled over, landing on the carpet. As the knife rose and fell over and over again, she didn't even pretend to feel the pain. She opened her bleeding mouth into a gaping hole and laughed—high-pitched, throaty cackles that made her head buck upon the limp wire of her neck. She'd given Orson one last gummy smile before the life snuffed from her eyes.

We've finally made a family, and nothing can go wrong.

The words stung his mind, made a riot of his thoughts, and his body shook as if he'd taken hold of a live electric wire. Maybe Gabriel wasn't touched by them. Maybe Gabriel was just a baby, an innocent, but for the sake of his promise to Martha he couldn't take that risk. For her he'd become a monster again. For her, he'd take the burden on himself and make the same impossible decision that he'd made back then.

"Goodbye, Gabriel. I love you. I'm sorry," he said, and he knew he meant every word.

The knife descended. A snap of ribs and then life drained from the line pressed into Gabriel's chest, red pouring in rivulets across his skin, his body drifting into stillness. Orson dropped the knife, crossed the hall to the bathroom and cleaned his hands off in the sink. Then, in his bedroom, he crawled into bed beside Martha and draped an arm around her.

When morning came, he would tell her about Gabriel. He'd also tell her about what had really happened with Michelle: how she had murdered his grandmother; how no one had kidnapped her like he'd sworn; and how he'd buried her in a trash bag stuffed with blankets and dropped her off at the local landfill before Martha returned from her spa vacation. This time there would be no deception. It would break Martha, but she deserved to know the truth. He'd let her decide what to think and then move on from there.

But for now, this one last night, he'd let her smile and sleep in the comfort of what ifs. Where she could dream of a happy, brighter future. Where their family was still safe, alive and whole. Where babies were just babies and parents their protectors, and nothing—nothing—would ever go wrong again.

SHE WHO WOULD RIP THE SKY ASUNDER

AFTER ARVIN'S ARGUMENT WITH Laura, the last thing he expected was a phone call from her daughter.

"My mom is hurt," said Wendy, her voice shrill, bordering on hysterics. "Help me, Arvin, I don't know what to do."

He didn't remember sprinting down the work steps to his car, the squeal of wheels pressing rubber tracks into the asphalt. Or the nine-mile drive, careening down the highway, his hand thumping the horn as if coaxing a heart back into life. He only began to track the world again when he pulled up to the curb in front of Laura's house, and felt the field of goosebumps swelling on his arms.

When he bullied through the front door, time lagged, the thought of hurrying so much faster than his body's willingness to comply.

"Wendy? Laura?"

No answer, so he searched the house. Doors opened on sluggish hinges and the other side of rooms retreated from his approach. All the stillness bolstered a sense of dread stalking the dark corners of his mind, until he couldn't help but shout to ease the mounting tension.

"Wendy? Laura? Answer me, goddamn it, somebody answer me!"

He charged out back and found Wendy huddled beneath the house's eaves. She was a doll of a girl, wearing a pink dress lined with lace, auburn hair done up in braids. Her dark complexion had been spoiled by a splash of blood that made her appearance bestial, like a tiger cub that had pressed its muzzle into a fresh bowl of viscera.

At the sight of her, Arvin stepped back and then gazed beyond the deck to the body lying in a bed of uncut grass. It was Laura. He scanned her for signs of life, some movement, a rise or fall of breath, however shallow. But he found nothing.

The world was taken over by a hush, everything warping like reflections in a funhouse mirror. He forgot to breathe, not that it mattered anymore. Nothing mattered because Laura was dead, and based on the meticulous wounds spread across her body, there could have only been one cause.

"Dear God," he said, rounding on Wendy, panic spreading like a wildfire through the brush of his insides. "What did you do?"

* * *

Arvin had met Laura two years prior through an online dating service his sister had recommended. The club and bar scene had never been his thing, and he wasn't the type to trawl work for romance on principle alone. That hadn't left many options, especially when compounded by his sister's constant pestering.

"It's how I met James and I couldn't be happier," she said during one of their bi-monthly phone conversations. James was her husband of two years, and not a conversation passed where she didn't brag on him for something. "You've been single for, what? Two years now? It's time you got back on that horse!"

"Horse, huh? To be clear, this isn't a site for animal fetishists, is it? 'Equine Romances: For a More Stable Relationship.'"

"Cute, Arvin. How's cute been working out for you?"

"All right, I'll do it," he said, a flush of embarrassment already spreading through his cheeks. "But if I end up with that lady from *Fatal Attraction*—"

"Glenn Close?"

"Right. If I end up with Glenn Close, it'll be on your head!"

That evening, he headed to his home office. Accounting for the block of time where his cat Orson made a mattress of his keyboard, it took him fifty minutes to finish writing up his profile. All the bright and shiny pieces of his personality condensed into a hundred-word blurb. It was depressing in a way he couldn't define, but he posted it anyway.

That was the easy part; the real chore came from waiting. After work, he'd log into his account and check his inbox. A red goose egg usually met his efforts—not including the handful of scammers promising nudes or sex for the right amount of personal information. But then Laura answered. She said she'd lived in town for a decade now. She liked to read, especially sci-fi and fantasy, and was half-Micronesian on her father's side. While Arvin hadn't a clue where Micronesia even was, that didn't keep him from admiring the results.

When can we meet? he wrote her, after a handful of email exchanges.

Saturday works, she wrote back, and sealed it with a smiley.

* * *

On their first date, they went the classic route: dinner and a movie. They had time for a five-minute chat before the theater lights cut out, and the screen lit their faces with fierce explosions, and the screaming palettes of distant worlds. Once in a while, they used that illumination to sneak glances at one another, followed by an awkward smile whenever the other noticed.

For dinner, they tried a new Italian spot downtown. Spaghetti and cream sodas followed, as well as pleasant—if mostly superficial—conversation. Eventually the subject of kids came up, on hindsight far less coincidentally than Arvin had perceived. He bravely led.

"I never wanted to be a father. I like kids, it's just..." He glanced around, absorbing the crowd of parents and their wriggling children. "They scream, they cry, they wet themselves. My friends say they love it, but I wonder. I really do."

He knew something was wrong when Laura started organizing her flatware into basic shapes, but realization only set in when he felt a solid chill with the meeting of their eyes.

"I have a kid," she said. "Her name is Wendy. She's seven and she means the world to me."

* * *

Despite the blunder of their first date, they went on many more. All of them went well, even on the odd occasion where teasing got the best of Laura and she reminded Arvin of the sour taste of his own foot. More dinners, museums, art galleries, and a haunted city walk went by before things became more serious.

"Let's have dinner at my place," she said, as he walked her to her car one night. "It'll be more comfortable for when you meet Wendy. She's a special girl, but shy to a fault, so don't be upset if she doesn't warm to you at first."

"Despite initial impressions, I'm actually good with kids. Cartoons and candy, am I right?"

Laura's smile was patient, if pitying. When the allotted day arrived, Arvin sauntered up Laura's doorstep with his hair parted and his collar choked by a silk black tie. She answered his knock and they briefly kissed.

"For you," he said, handing her a rose.

"That's adorable," she said, turning her attention behind the door. "Wendy, there's someone here I want you to meet."

Wendy slid into view. She squirmed into the protective space beneath her mother's arm before pinching the fringes of her skirt and giving Arvin a tilted curtsey.

"So you're Wendy?" He held up a small box of chocolates. "These are for you."

She shot a glance up at her mother before she took it, her expression doubtful, unimpressed. Throughout dinner, she didn't say a word. Whenever Arvin tried to draw her into the conversation, she would tuck her chin into her chest and stir the contents of her plate until his attention shifted elsewhere. After dinner, Laura cleared the dishes. As she headed for the kitchen, Arvin leaned in close to her and said, "Can Wendy have my present for dessert?"

Laura shrugged. "Ask her."

He turned to Wendy, her expression as unimpressed as ever. "Well?"

Wendy's eyebrows furrowed as she slipped the lid off the box, revealing four cordials set in a dark brown plastic tray. She took one, cupped it in her hand, let her fingers do a rhythmic dance above it. Her movements were too quick for Arvin to follow, but by the time she'd finished, the chocolate had split in two, and its cherry rested like a twin beside the hollow marble of its peel.

"That's some trick," said Arvin, gaping. "How'd you do that?"

"Thank you," she said, ignoring the question. "I don't like chocolate, but that was fun."

* * *

Arvin succumbed to domesticated bliss, spending most of his free time at Laura's. In return, she gave him a spot for his toiletries, his own side of the bed, and use of the second closet in her bedroom. He knew the latter was a sacrifice. Her penchant for organization bordered on OCD, and the way she had to cram her things into a single closet hurt her in ways he could only guess at.

On their first anniversary, they talked about their future together, what it meant and where it was progressing.

"You're here all the time anyway," she said. "Why don't you move in?"

"Really? Orson too? I thought you hated cats."

"We'll make it work."

He expected to feel a backlash, the equivalent of stampeding elephants trumpeting a warning in his ear. Instead, there was calm, all the pieces of a puzzle sliding into place.

"What about Wendy?"

"She told me she's fine with it, but it wouldn't hurt if you asked her permission."

Violent winds had cracked a few boughs off the goliath oaks that skirted the edges of the back yard, big as trees themselves, though of a lesser order. Wendy lay upon the lawn, arms and legs askew, doing her best impression of a fallen branch. Her attention was focused on a cloud, an island cumulonimbus that seemed to drop its shadow clear across the town.

"Hello," Arvin said.

Wendy waved. As her concentration increased, her eyes flared, and her mouth pinched shut like a baby refusing to be fed. He got to his knees and eased back against the ground beside her.

"Your mom and I—"

"Shush. I'm trying to feel the cloud."

"What?"

She heaved a sigh, as if the effort of responding were too much to bother with. "I'm trying to see how it fits together and if you keep distracting me, I—" She turned to him, fixing a mean glare against his face. "Forget it," she said, and climbed to her feet.

"Wendy, wait."

"No. I'm mad at you."

"But—"

"Yes, fine. You can live with us," she said.

He heaved a sigh of his own and chuckled, trailing Wendy back inside. When he reached the deck, sunlight broke into the yard and he glanced into the sky. The cloud had split in two, both halves drifting in opposite directions, revealing a flat expanse from where they once were joined. He stared through the glass of the patio door at Wendy—now seated at the dining table, already scribbling on a sheet of paper—and then back into sky.

It had to be a coincidence, some natural phenomenon he'd never seen before. Still, a part of him couldn't help but wonder.

* * *

Months of familiarity had cracked the shell off Wendy's introversion, and she clamored for Arvin's attention at all hours of the day. He began to dread the minutes after he came home, when she would greet him at the door, chattering like a squirrel over whatever minutia had caught her interest. That evening, Laura surprised him when she met him at the door instead. Her face had the look of a crudely carved bust, with red-rimmed eyes, and black mascara tears running down her cheeks.

She choked a greeting, and then said, "Come with me."

He didn't know what to expect when she led him down the hall, into her office. Wendy stood in one corner, stiff and straight as a board pressed against the wall. The carpet was mottled with dark spots, and in the middle of the room a green towel was draped over a mound surrounded by a slick, red stain.

"Wendy," Laura said, in the too-calm voice of someone who was anything but.

Wendy turned to Arvin. Deep lines formed around her mouth, with tendrils of saliva strung across the edges of her lips. "Sorry, Arvin."

"What's going on?" he said.

The anguish on Laura and Wendy's faces only worsened, and he turned his attention to the enigma of the mound. Vague suspicions ratcheted into sudden understanding as he inched closer, each step shortened by indecision, an unwillingness to confirm the narrative forming in his mind. He snatched the towel up, and slapped a hand over his mouth, but was unable to suppress the strangled moan that followed.

Orson lay in pieces. His organs had been removed and placed in piles beside the segments of his limbs and hollow trunk. Only a black sheet of his pelt remained intact, draped across the carpet like a lion skin rug. The muscles of one of Orson's legs contracted. Arvin averted his eyes to Wendy, and she withered at his stare.

"I'm sorry," she said again. "I was only trying to see how he worked, but Mom shouted, and I got distracted, and...I accidentally undid him."

She toddled forward, arms outstretched. He almost didn't hug her, but vulnerability leaked from her every pore and he couldn't help thinking of a helpless lamb, throwing itself before the mercy of the butcher. He bit down on the inside of his cheek, pushing the maelstrom of anger and sadness deep inside.

"You undid him?" he whispered in her ear. "Like the cloud?"

She pressed a solemn nod into his chest. Once he bore the needles of her touch for as long as he could stand, he stepped back.

"I need time to think," he said. "About everything."

Laura couldn't stop nodding; Wendy couldn't stop crying. Arvin stumbled to the entryway, refusing to look back until the barrier of the front door slammed shut between them.

* * *

The next morning, Arvin, Wendy, and Laura assembled in the back yard. While Laura and Wendy watched, Arvin dug a five-foot hole and shoved a plastic trash bag containing Orson's parts inside it. He spoke a few words and then they dispersed, to mourn in separate places.

From that day forward, Laura never broached the subject of Orson's death again, choosing to feign geniality, as if a pert smile and silly jokes would somehow mend the broken bonds between them. Wendy took the opposite approach. Melancholy and self-loathing clung to her like a second skin. She spent the brunt of her days hiding in her bedroom, sobbing, and emerged only for school and mealtimes.

As for Arvin, he leaned on Laura for emotional support, even as he bided his time gathering evidence on Wendy, some "ah-ha" moment that would nudge his vague conjectures into undeniable facts. Something profoundly odd was going on with her, and he intended to find out what. For weeks nothing happened, so he was forced to take matters into his own hands.

"We need to talk about Wendy," he said at bedtime, after another day of awkward lulls and almost-conversations.

Laura lay on her side of the bed, facing the window, unmoving. The threadbare rays of moonlight pouring through their curtains did nothing to disturb the darkness. He wasn't sure she was even awake until she turned to him, and warm breath blanketed his ear.

"I knocked on her door this afternoon," she said. "She wouldn't answer, so I used an emergency key. You should have seen her face when I came in, red and swollen and twisted by rage. She screamed at me and then pushed me out. That's not like her. She's never done that before."

"Maybe she and I should talk, alone, and find a way to put all this behind us?"

"Do you think it'd work?"

He shrugged, a useless gesture in the pervading dark. "Couldn't be worse than this."

* * *

Arvin brought Wendy to the local park on Main Street. It was more a field of grass, with a single whitewashed bench set like an afterthought in its center. Douglas firs tossed shade over the vicinity while a sandpit lay like a forgotten promise of a slide and swing.

Arvin took a seat on the bench, and Wendy slid—arms crossed—into the opposite corner. For a time, they sat in silence: Arvin practicing his words, and Wendy studying her shoes as if a novel were written on them.

"I think it's time we cleared the air," he said at last.

Wendy's legs began to shake, her pigtails swaying like a lazy pair of car wipers. "I'm sorry, Arvin," she said. "I'm sorry, sorry, sorry."

"That's not what I mean. Look, Wendy, you may shred chocolates into tiny bits on purpose, but I don't think you would... Let's just say I know Orson was an accident."

"You do?" she said, meeting his gaze at last.

"Of course. You're not an evil girl. I never believed that for a second."

She smiled. A wet sheen spread over her eyes before she turned away again.

"What do you mean when you say you 'undid' something? How does it work? Do you have any control over it?"

"Mom says I'm not supposed to talk about that. She says it's impossible and the sooner I admit that, the sooner I'll stop blaming others for my mistakes."

"How long has she known about it?"

"Since it started. Years."

He paused to consider her answer. Did Laura truly know about Wendy's gift, or had her previous "mistakes" been a lot more inconspicuous? And what kind of trouble would he get into by ignoring Laura's wishes? It could put a crimp in their relationship, maybe even end things. Still, doing nothing seemed reckless, irresponsible, maybe even murder by omission if the circumstances worsened.

"I don't want you to disobey your mother," said Arvin. "But if you can do what you think you can do—"

"I can!"

"Then show me."

She squared up her shoulders, then dropped onto her knees to root around the ground behind the bench.

"Don't do the bench," said Arvin.

"I know."

"Or the bench's legs."

"I know, I know."

Soon, she bounced back into view, an arm raised high in triumph. Between her fingers she held a pill bug, already rolled into a ball.

"Now what?" he asked.

"Now watch."

She held her breath. Her eyes widened, her cheeks went flush, and then the pill bug began to unfold. Instead of straightening, revealing a cluster of legs scrabbling for purchase, the segments of the pill bug's shell began to peel.

Its limbs and eyestalks detached next before Arvin said, "That's enough. Can you put it back together?"

She shook her head, a wet sheen returning to her eyes. "No, I...I just focused enough to undo it, like you said."

"That's okay." He took her hand, dumped the stagnate lump that remained of the bug onto his palm. He dropped it to the ground and crushed it beneath his heel—a mercy killing if he'd ever seen one. "What if you had memorized the connections? Could you have reassembled it then?"

"I don't know."

"How about you give it a try?"

She nodded and then dropped to the ground, to root out another bug.

* * *

Going to the park became a regular part of Arvin and Wendy's daily routine. After work, he'd pick her up from home. They'd say goodbye to Laura and then load up the car with supplies: mostly an assortment of bugs they'd captured, for when wild ones were hard to come by; a folding table to make the undoing and reassembling tidier; and a wire-mesh box with a cardboard lid, for days when heavy winds threatened to blow the pieces of their "test subjects" away.

"You're getting better," said Arvin, during an early evening session. "At this rate, you'll be tearing down and putting mountains back together."

"That'd be cool," Wendy said, watching a little black spider she reassembled crawl along her hand. "Once I know how something works, it's easy to fix. It's almost like they want to be whole."

"How do you mean?"

"It's hard to explain."

"Please, master," Arvin said, palming a fist. "Your humble student wishes to understand your wisdom!"

She tried to frown, but the corners of her mouth betrayed her with a smile. "It's like there's a...thing between them and it pulls them back together. Like they know where they're supposed to be and won't rest until they are. All I have to do is...nudge them a little, to get it started."

She turned to him, her eyes round and bright as searchlights.

Now it was his turn to shrug. "Birds don't know how they fly, they just can."

"I don't get it."

"Never mind."

For the most part, Laura seemed fine with Wendy's extracurricular activities. So long as Wendy's mood improved, Laura didn't ask questions. And it did improve. The many days and nights Wendy had spent brooding in quiet isolation were finished. She now joined mealtimes without complaint, smiled often, and didn't hesitate to interject in conversations. For all intents and purposes, she was her normal self again.

"Looks like daddy-daughter time is going well," Laura said while lying in bed with Arvin.

The three of them had spent the last hours of the night playing board games, something Wendy had taken to calling "Family Night." They'd capped it off with pizza and a movie before Wendy turned in. Already, her punctuating snores barreled through the hallway like a Big Wheel trike.

"Daddy?" said Arvin. He smiled, or at least he thought he did; he wasn't awake enough to know for sure. "I think she thinks of me more as a friend."

"It was a joke. Seeing you two get along is all that matters. No need to put a label on it."

"See? Kids love me."

"But do you love her?"

The bluntness of the question startled him, hauling him back from the precipice of sleep. He'd never thought of Wendy that way before. He cared for her, and sacrificed a lot of free time for the sake of her health and well-being. But if not for the fear that she might do to Laura what she'd done to Orson, he'd still be holding her at arm's length. Another person's child. Someone else's problem.

"I don't know. Maybe?"

"Let me put it like this. If you never got a chance to see her again, would that be okay with you?"

He shook his head. "No. It wouldn't."

"That makes me," she yawned, "glad."

Laura drifted off. The master snorer began practicing her art, with Wendy the apprentice adding tenor notes to their bedtime symphony. Arvin felt too awake to join them. The quickness of his answer surprised him, and coupled with his emphatic tone, he knew he'd meant it.

* * *

On Arvin's way to work, he paused before a corner jewelry shop. Not a mass chain, but a Mom and Pop operation, the kind small enough to stuff into the corner of a garage and still have room for parking. He stared at the engagement rings that took up the brunt of their front window display, picturing Laura, a ring glinting from her finger, hand held out to admire it from afar. Then his imagination truly soared, and he envisioned them walking down the center aisle of some little rustic church, following a path of rose petals left behind by Wendy. While he and Laura had never talked marriage before, the pull of dropping to one knee and proffering a velvet box had never been stronger.

For the remainder of his shift, more variations of a wedding theme occupied his mind. Not as a distraction, but filling up the cracks of idle thoughts, the way good things do. And why not? His relationship with Laura and Wendy had surpassed his expectations. Maybe it was time to take the next step, see how it resonated with Laura, and maybe make her "daddy-daughter" comment true.

The moment he got home that evening, he intended to do just that, but was startled when he found Laura waiting for him in the entryway. Fear turned his limbs to rubber and locking his knees was the only thing that kept him standing.

"What's wrong?" he said. "Are you hurt? Where's Wendy?"

"I'm fine. As for Wendy, you and I had better talk."

Laura's body was a large-print tome of discontent: arms folded, eyebrows furrowed, her mouth pinched and sagging. She motioned to the couch, but made a point to put distance in-between them, a cushion wide.

"I found Wendy crying in the back yard today, cradling a blue jay. She said it'd crashed into an upstairs window and broke its neck. She said it wasn't what it looked like, that she hadn't hurt it. She was trying to fix it, and you were the one who gave her permission."

Arvin's mouth went dry. "I can explain."

"Good. I hope to God you can, for everybody's sake."

"You remember how she was," Arvin said, leaning away to gain some distance from her smoldering anger. "Taking all the blame for what had happened to Orson, internalizing it, letting it tear her apart. She said it was an accident, and I, for one, believe her."

He hesitated. What he meant to say next sounded like insanity, the ravings of a man abandoned too long with only his own thoughts. Despite the evidence pinned and labeled in the glass case of his mind, a part of him still wanted to deny it. He'd spent many sleepless nights coming to terms with this strange new vision of reality. How was he supposed to convince Laura in minutes?

"What's more," he continued, "I've seen it! I've watched her use her gift many times over, and it's the most incredible thing to witness."

"Okay, you're done."

"I know how this sounds, but see it for yourself. Let her show you what she can do."

"I said enough! It's my turn now. When she told me what was going on, I'd hoped it was a misunderstanding, that you were humoring her, trying to ease her back into a healthy state of mind. Instead, you've convinced her she's some kind of superhero, and that none of the things she's done were her fault. That's not just bewildering, it's *dangerous.*"

She passed a sleeve beneath her eyes, her lip trembling. "Hurt me, and I'll give you a few more chances. I'm strong; I can handle it. But hurt her, and there's no forgiveness for that."

"I know I was wrong," he said, and reached to drop a hand onto her knee. "But I did what I thought was right. You didn't believe her. She needed someone, and I was all she had."

"I'm her mother!" she shouted, jabbing a finger at his chest. "I'm the one who gets to decide what's best for her!"

"That's not fair."

"And pretending like you're Professor Xavier to her X-men is?"

"At least I tried. What have you done?"

The fury that poured from Laura's face was a violent thing. Arvin flinched, almost certain her gaze could tear him apart as easily as Wendy's.

"You know," she said, "I didn't think I had the strength to do this, but you made it easy. We're done."

"Laura—"

"Please leave, Arvin."

He slinked toward the exit, unable to risk another glance at Laura for fear of what he might see lodged in her expression. Before he left, he glanced down the hallway, toward Wendy's bedroom door.

"There's no excuse," he said, hoping she could hear him. "It's *my* fault. *I'm* the adult. I should have known better." And then, to no one in particular, "For what it's worth, I really am sorry."

* * *

He went to work the next day, thinking a distraction would do him good. He was wrong. For the majority of his shift, he stayed locked inside his office, cheeks wedged between the vise grip of his fists, and his elbows propped against his desktop.

He told himself that Laura was just punishing him, and any minute he'd hear her special ringtone chiming from his pocket, and all his fears and insecurities would fade away. He even practiced what he would say, unwilling to give his tongue free reign after the travesty of last night. When his cell finally rang, with Laura's home number pasted on its screen, he nearly doubled over in relief.

"I was beginning to think you'd never call," he said.

At first there was silence. Then Wendy's voice spilled from the receiver. She had to repeat herself several times before his arm lost strength, the phone clattered to the floor, and his mind went numb with sudden understanding.

My mom is hurt. Help me, Arvin, I don't know what to do.

* * *

Adrenaline surged through Arvin as he examined Laura's body lying in the grass amid a pool of her own blood. Deep cuts covered her from head to foot, strips of flesh unwinding like a half-peeled orange. How he wished this were a game, that she'd sit up, alive and well, and grinning like a jack-o'-lantern.

"Don't you ever lie to me again," she'd say as she tore off her prosthetics.

And he wouldn't. The idea would never cross his mind if she'd only stir, if she'd only breathe, and make this prank complete.

"Answer me," he said to Wendy. "What happened?"

Wendy looked drained, her eyes like soulless glass pushed too deep inside her tiger-cub face. "I undid her."

"On purpose?"

Her bottom lip trembled. "We fought."

He fell to his knees beside her, nestling her hands between his own. "Wendy, did you do this on purpose?"

"No. I didn't realize what was happening until it was too late."

Arvin took a breath and held it until his lungs felt hot and bloated. He thought about the scant options available to him: calling the police, an ambulance, a doctor that made house calls. But every one of them would be worthless for repairing the damage Wendy had already done. It could even make things worse. No one would believe the circumstances told a story of anything short of murder, and whether they blamed him or Wendy, their lives together would be over.

"Your mother," he said. "Can you save her?"

"It's too hard."

"You once ripped a cloud in two and didn't break a sweat, and the bugs you reassembled weren't exactly Lego sets."

"It's like the blue jay; it's been too long. When I nudged her parts they barely moved, and even if I could force them back, I don't know how they're supposed to fit."

"Then use me."

"What do you mean?"

"Undo me. Memorize the connections. Use me like a blueprint to fix her."

"It doesn't work that way."

"You won't know unless you try."

She studied him, narrowed her eyes, pursed her lips. He felt a brief tickle in his chest, but then her face relaxed and the feeling vanished too.

"No! What if I kill you? I'll be alone. Please don't make me do it, Arvin."

"If you don't at least try, that knowledge will stay with you for the rest of your life." He took her hand and squeezed it. "I know you. You'll never forgive yourself."

"I'm scared," she said, and threw her arms around him, drenching his shirt with a fresh stream of tears. "I love you, Arvin."

"I love you too."

He meant the words to console her. But the idea gathered force, sliding seamlessly into an excavated part of him that had been forming for months. Those countless hours they'd spent together had never been a burden. The excitement of discovery—the sheer awe of witnessing true miracles—had helped, but it was more than that. He did love Wendy, and that realization made him hug her all the harder.

"Listen to me," he said. "You can do this."

Wendy nodded and Arvin swallowed hard, lowering himself to the deck. As he lay there, staring at patterns in the overhanging branches, he wondered if the pain of being undone would be as brutal as being vivisected with a knife. The answer came faster than he expected.

Wendy went flush with deep concentration and the tickle in his chest returned, stronger than before. His fingers numbed, separated from his hands, a few sliding down his chest and resting like limp, fat grubs beside him. Far from pain, he felt a sense of otherness about them, as if they weren't his own, or he was watching it happen to a character on TV.

The numbness spread throughout his body. The flesh of his arms, torso, and legs began to unravel like ribbon from a spool. Joints unlocked, muscles unfurled, and pieces of him dropped away until he could feel little more than the substance of his own thoughts.

Focus, he wanted to say, but his tongue no longer functioned, and the stirring in his throat only produced a growl. The trees and sky faded into black as his eyes detached and rolled away. *You can do this*, he tried to think, but his mind drifted into nothing, and all he could do was acquiesce, give himself to the void that swallowed him piece by disconnected piece.

* * *

He had brief glimpses of awareness, images and sensations that didn't make much sense. Wet warmth brushed his cheeks and lips. He felt his body lift before being set upon a cloud. A stern face peered down at him from some incalculable distance and a thousand dangling, needle-thin fingers swept across his face.

When he opened his eyes again, he found himself lying on the couch in the living room, his head resting on Laura's lap. He held still, convinced that if he moved the spell would break, rendering the lap into a pillow and the rest of Laura into some unlikely mix of couch, curtain, and shadow. Then she said, "There you are," and he knew she was real.

He tried to move, wanted to shout and embrace her, but the pull of gravity crushed him against the cushions.

"You," he said, the edges of his mouth twitching, trying to be a smile.

She laughed. "Yes. Me."

"Then..."

"It worked. Wendy fixed me and then fixed you."

"Where is she?"

"In bed. Apparently Frankensteining two adults is taxing for a little girl. As soon as her head touched her pillow, she was lost to the world. Lights out."

"So you believe us now?"

"She basically hauled me up and made me watch. I saw her pull you together, saw your blood flow back inside you like she'd pressed the reverse button on some cosmic remote control. So, yeah, I'm definitely a believer."

"But? What aren't you telling me?"

Her eyes rolled up to stare into the ceiling. She shook her head. "I don't understand it. Her father was a do-nothing drunk, and I can barely move the couch enough to vacuum underneath it. How does she do these things, Arvin? What is she?"

"She's Wendy."

"That's not what I mean."

"I know, but that's what matters. Maybe one day she'll be more, a contractor who can build houses, or whole skyscrapers, in record time. A weather person with accurate predictions, a surgeon whose every patient recovers, or maybe something greater than you and I can imagine. Let her decide that when the time comes and, for now, let her be a little girl. Our little girl."

"Excuse me?" Laura said, raising an eyebrow.

"I mean, if you say yes."

"To what?"

"Go easy." He coughed, the closest to a laugh he could muster. "I just died today."

"If you recall, I died too. That puts us on even ground." She tapped a finger against his chest. "So if you want to say something meaningful about our relationship, you got to use your words, mister."

"Marry me."

"Do you mean it? After everything you've seen, after all you've been through, you're sure that's what you want?"

"Yes."

Her whole face lit up with a grin and she pulled him closer so that their lips almost touched. "Then that's my answer, too," she said, and sealed it with a kiss.

PENELOPE'S SONG

PENELOPE GAZED THROUGH HER bedroom window, mesmerized by the motion of the night. Flowers trembled, grass ruffled, and trees swayed, flailing their branches. The sight of it unsettled her. In fifteen years, she hadn't learned much about the world, but she did know this: when the wind was absent like it was tonight, a garden wasn't supposed to move an inch. It could only mean one thing; the Gnasher had returned.

It had come on twelve occasions over the last few months. Each time, the wail of an ambulance followed where men in blue uniforms hustled covered gurneys out of sight. And each time, the neighborhood around Penelope's group home became one voice quieter, one life poorer, and the nights that much less enchanting. But there was a quality about the Gnasher that terrified her even more than the certainty of pain and death—a sense that it didn't belong, that it was an intruder. She imagined it folding its spine in half, so that its two ends met, and scuttling on hands and feet through the black line of the horizon. From darkness, into the light of our world.

No sooner had she thought it than the sound of grinding teeth poured through her dirt-encrusted screen. The noise skirted along the perimeter of her house, pausing by each window, as if the Gnasher were scrutinizing the sleeping housemates within. Before it could draw nearer to Penelope's window, she sunk to the floor and, with her back pressed into the wall, shielded her eyes with her hands.

Had it seen her? She didn't know for sure, but by the way it passed her, without a change in the cadence of its grinding, she had to guess it hadn't. It retreated beyond the distant corner of the yard, toward her neighbors' homes. Only then did she feel safe enough to scramble for the underside of her table.

Somewhere in the distance, the Gnasher grunted. Any moment now it would find a new victim and its grinding would transform into an elated clack. Penelope wished she could stop it, but she didn't have the strength or temerity to fight it. Shouting a warning wasn't an option either; the mental haze that had trapped her words away since childhood allowed only an incoherent mumble. And so, she squinched within the safety of her hiding place, counting down the seconds, her heart thumping in sync with the ticking of her wall clock.

She cried. Low at first, and then harder, louder, as months of pent-up guilt and anger churned the contents of her stomach. Her insides bloated, full and round. The sensation slid fat as a bowling ball into her chest and exploded from her mouth—not as the vomit she expected, but a discordant sound, a single riotous note.

"I hear you, little songbird," the Gnasher said between labored breaths, its voice pained, almost peevish.

A vicious crack, like alligator jaws snapping shut, and the peal of grinding teeth trailed off. The Gnasher had fled. Back into the black line of the horizon.

The very idea that she had scared it off left Penelope stunned and silent. Hours passed before she even thought to leave the underside of the table. With a quick glance out the window, to ensure it had truly gone, she climbed into bed and fell into a deep and lasting sleep.

* * *

Penelope opened her eyes to find Old Woman stooped and pacing, picking through the worst of the bedroom's disarray. Old Woman shoved picture books onto their shelves, dropped scattered toys back into their storage box, stowed dirty clothes inside the hamper, and propped Penelope's favorite teddy bear—which had been set beside the door, to guard against intrusion—upon the dresser.

"I don't get paid enough for this," Old Woman said. "Every day it's the same thing, crash and clutter, crash and clutter."

And she was right. It embarrassed Penelope to realize how seldom she kept her room clean. Last night was no excuse. Even on days when the Gnasher didn't come, she always got too caught up in something to remember. She tried mouthing an apology, but Old Woman was too preoccupied to notice.

When the room had been restored to some semblance of order, Old Woman turned to Penelope at last.

"Look who decided to join the waking world," she said, adjusting the wrinkles of her face into a smile. "You don't look so good. Didn't you sleep well?"

Penelope shook her head.

"I heard you were a noisy goose last night. Some neighbors complained about your shrieking. You know that's against the rules, right?"

Penelope tried to explain what happened. She motioned to the window, tracing the shape of what she imagined the Gnasher looked like with her hands. To simulate a mouth, she splayed her fingers, curled them like claws, and slammed her palms together.

"Do you understand me?" said Old Woman, ignoring Penelope's gesticulations. She caterwauled, jabbed a finger at her throat and shook her head. "Off limits. Okay?"

Penelope bit her lip and nodded.

* * *

She took a quick shower before hurrying to breakfast. Discontented chatter filled the narrow walls of the dining room as staff arranged the residents around the table. Penelope sat on her favorite chair and of her own volition; it was something she took pride in.

Most of the residents couldn't dress, use the facilities, or even eat without someone's help. Penelope often had to wait for staff to pacify the others before she got her own fair share of attention. Still, her relative autonomy came with its own intangible benefits: it felt nice to be a shining light for once when most of her life she'd always been called a good-for-nothing, a chore, and... What was that word her parents had liked to use? Helpless.

"Hello, Penelope!" Brown-Haired Girl said with an eager smile. "You ready to eat?"

Penelope couldn't help herself; she laughed, twining her fingers into knots. It was unusual to feel happy during daytime, but Brown-Haired Girl's smile was always so infectious. If it wasn't for the fact that she didn't come around too often, Penelope thought they would have been the best of friends.

Old Woman pounded through the swinging kitchen door, smoke and the pungent scent of orange cleaner drifting in behind her. Mean followed next, an ample woman Penelope knew for her crooked teeth and hostile disposition. Once they passed out meals, Old Woman said, "You have a new housemate." She pointed to the end of the table where a new boy sat, his eyes wide, his body shaking like a rabbit in a wolves' den. "His name is Franklin. Everyone say, 'Hello, Franklin'!"

Penelope formed the words with her lips, but besides her, no one else even tried. In response, Franklin's eyelids fell into crescents as he grinned and waved at her, his hand a blur of motion.

* * *

Penelope spent the afternoon on the back porch, draped across a lawn chair beneath the shadow of the eaves. Though she appeared relaxed, the weary glaze over her eyes revealed her true feelings. She hated daylight. With all her neighbors gone, emptiness and quiet hovered like a fine mist over her back yard, reminding her of the solitude she felt no matter where she went.

No, what she really loved was night. That was when her neighbors returned from work or school, and with them came that electric surge of energy that made her feel alive. Because when darkness blotted out the space between them, and their windows shined bright as searchlights, she could pretend to be a part of their homes, a friend in their midst. Someone who belonged.

But it only came after sundown, and now even those sacred hours were spoiled by the Gnasher's murderous intrusions. While the sun plodded across the sky, the twinge in her chest unfolded into a shiver. For once, she dreaded night almost as much as she longed for it.

* * *

Penelope awoke with a gasp and gazed through her bedroom window. It was sometime in the still-dark morning and a storm had crept across the sky. Raindrops pattered her rooftop and the trees rustled in harmony with the whistling wind. But it wasn't the placid song of nature that had startled her awake; the sound had been more violent, like broken glass scattered across pavement, or snapping bones, or...

She threw herself from bed, stumbled to the open window. On the left-hand side, beyond the chain-link fence that marked the border of her property, the slivered yards of townhouses lay wrapped in utter darkness. To the right stood a motel-style apartment complex, its solitary light buzzing and winking at her from the wall above the walkway. She held her breath, shifting her attention in a sweeping gaze from one back to the other, hoping beyond all hope that her ears had been mistaken.

The din intensified. Rain faltered and the wind ebbed, as if the world itself had been frightened into dormancy. A sudden hush fell across the yard, boosting that solitary sound so that it echoed in her ears, crawled beneath her skin, inhabited her mind. Finally, the source of the disturbance revealed itself. Two half-transparent figures skulked through the grass alley between her neighbors' homes, their outlines dancing with the suppleness of flames. One was a hulking brute with legs thick and round as tree trunks, and a stomach like a bulging sack. The other was a cadaverous thing, with arms as long as poles, whisking its jaw from side to side in the Gnasher's telltale clatter.

The Gnasher vaulted over the chain-link fence and the Brute followed after, clearing the top rail in a single stride. Once in Penelope's back yard, the Gnasher pointed a too-long finger in her direction.

"I see you, little songbird," it said.

She could almost feel the dagger-edge of its nail press into her skull. While she had been scared before, this time fear consumed her. The air grew thick and stagnant; a shiver rooted to her spine. An animal impulse flared inside her, but she didn't have time to obey the urge to flee, or even think. Her mouth opened into a perfect O and the riotous note from before returned, blasting through her window screen with savage fury.

The Gnasher gripped the lawn, its stub legs wavering behind it like a flag caught in a gale. The brute squatted, anchoring its legs deep into the ground, shielding its face with its arms. They held out for a minute longer, but then the Gnasher was swept away and the Brute collapsed, flattening the fence as the swollen boulder of its body tumbled out of sight. Yet still Penelope sang. She had to be sure they were gone for good, for everybody's sake.

Somewhere close by—she couldn't see quite where—a window banged open.

"Shut up, shut up, shut up! It's three in the goddamn morning!"

* * *

She was already awake by the time Old Woman arrived. She had been so happy with herself, so proud of her accomplishment, that she couldn't sleep for long. And so, she had simply lain in bed and waited for the sunrise, her face etched with a beatific smile.

Old Woman didn't return the smile. If anything, she looked irritated, evincing a spirit that reminded Penelope of Mean.

"You did it again, girl. Now Boss Man's involved and he's not happy."

Penelope sank into her bed, pulling the covers up to hide her frown. Old Woman's tone was coarse. Not nasty or spiteful, but unpleasant in its own way.

"They're threatening to send you packing. He don't want trouble, and it's not like we agree, but it's the neighbors. They won't stand for you shouting out the window at all hours of the night, okay? Those are the rules." Old Woman pointed to her throat and shook her head. "Understand?"

Penelope nodded. She understood, of course, but the thought of obeying sent a chill writhing down her spine.

* * *

After breakfast, Penelope retired to the rec room. She made straight for the bookshelf beside the whitewashed fireplace and grabbed her favorite game, Chutes and Ladders. Holding the box's lid out, she paced around her housemates, hoping the vibrant image on the cover would entice someone to play.

Curly Hair sat on the tile by the entryway, so preoccupied with a plain rubber ball she didn't even steal a glance. When Penelope walked in front of the TV, Fists and Frown waved her aside and shouted, "Move!" Blank reclined in her electric wheelchair, arms draped over her lap, facing the sliding glass door. But a cautious look at her expression showed she was in no condition to care about anything.

She tried Brown-Haired Girl and Old Woman last. "Maybe later," they said. She didn't get her hopes up, though. The way they returned so quickly to their conversation, she knew "later" would be a long time coming.

Penelope lowered to her knees in the center of the carpet, unfolded the board, and placed the spinner by its side. She took three pieces in blue plastic stands and positioned them on squares where the pictures of little boys and girls were happiest. Then she watched their taunting stillness with a sigh. It was just as well no one wanted to play with her. She didn't know how to anyway.

* * *

Penelope withered in the summer heat, amid brooding trees and plants drooping with exhaustion. Across the way, a cat prowled the devastation of the fence, its attention fixed on a blue jay dropping oblivious caws into the grass. She pretended to track its progress, even smiled when it dashed too soon and began to lick its paw—as if scaring the bird away had always been its intention. But really, her mind was preoccupied with the new boy, Franklin. She watched him from the corner of her eye as he meandered through the back yard, towing doting parents close behind him. It was the second time they'd visited that week.

A jealous ache filled her up to bursting. She had no idea how long it had been since she'd last seen her own parents: a month, maybe even a year now? She could remember the last time they were together, how they hugged her, kissed her, and darted glances in her direction that were uncommonly adoring. Before bedtime, Daddy had read her more than one story and Mommy had even sung a lullaby. Both tucked her in to bed that night, their hands careful and deliberate, as if they were cocooning her in the safety of their own shadows. She remembered the easy way she fell asleep, a smile tugging at her cheeks that she thought might last forever.

But by daybreak everything had changed. Suddenly, they couldn't meet her eyes and couldn't speak to her without their voices trembling. They packed the car up with a few of her things, drove her to the group home, and brought her inside without a word of explanation. After her parents retreated to the porch, they watched her screaming, struggling to escape Mean's meaty grasp. Mommy cried and Daddy's furrowed brows cast shadows over his watering eyes. Not long after, they left her behind and never returned again.

It had taken hours before the night came, blotting out her sadness along with the sunlight. She'd never enjoyed another daytime since.

* * *

Penelope gazed through her window, her chin resting on her hand, letting another night wrap its cozy arms around her. It wasn't just a microcosm out there, it was a micro-cosmos. Lamps and track lights beamed like suns and stars, vacant houses roiled with the blackness of empty space, and Penelope—the solitary planet, the lonely sphere—orbited it all.

She listened as musicians strummed acoustic guitars, as televisions blared, and housemates shared quick banter or ardent conversations. With eyes closed, she soaked it in, trying to pin understanding on it, trying to connect with that peaceful incoherence. Sometimes she laughed, picturing what her neighbors were doing, imagining she was a face in their crowd. When shadows and silhouettes flung out in plain sight, she even pressed her palm up to the window screen, pretending she could feel their owner's warmth.

But as the night dragged on, the noise settled into murmurs. Televisions shut off, guests scurried to their own homes, and even the musicians conceded to the waning hours. One by one each light winked out, spreading darkness until only Penelope's lamp remained.

It wasn't long before a new noise broke the silence, emerging from the horizon with slowly mounting vigor. It sounded like wolves howling, albeit tainted, unnatural in a way she couldn't hear, but felt in the pit of her quivering stomach. The moon buzzed with distress. The trees and flowers of her garden jerked from side to side, as if they were trying to uproot themselves to escape the coming madness.

Penelope felt dizzy listening to it, but for once not overwhelmed. She knew how to deal with these things and she no longer felt afraid. Her mouth drew a circle, her stomach inflated— but just as she was about to let the song loose, she remembered Old Woman's warning. If she sang again she'd be in trouble. What did that mean? Her imagination did its best to fill in the missing pieces.

She pictured Mean dragging her to a car, locking her in the backseat and taking her to a strange place where she would be left behind. That's what people did when they didn't want you anymore.

Penelope threw herself to the floor and rolled beneath the table. She thought the howling had increased, joined by a timid whimper, only to realize the latter had come from her mouth. Somehow that was worse, a sign of how powerless she'd become.

The Intruders stormed the grass alley, their feet stomping with the potency of thunder. She hoped it would be loud enough to wake the neighbors—just this once—and they'd be able to protect themselves, leaving her free to hide. But nothing human squeaked above the clamor. She alone knew. She alone heard.

They passed the shambles of the fence separating the yards. A second more and they were beside the window of her sanctuary, her very room. She heard moans, snivels, sighs, hisses, and hollow tinny whispers, all distinct and yet riding on the same air of malevolence.

They passed through her window screen and, for the first time, Penelope saw them clearly. Even if she could have formulated a description, words fell short of the reality. Crooked, bent, scarred, ugly, writhing—each term no better than a child's doodle. The urge to sing grew strong within her. Her gut bloated, her throat widened, and only lodging a fist deep into her mouth kept the song from rising.

The Gnasher pushed through the gathered crowd. It sunk down beside Penelope's hiding place and thrust its face forward; fever warmth radiated from its skin against her ear. "Where's your voice now, little songbird?" the Gnasher said, slicing her cheek with the tip of its nail.

The others tittered with amusement. As if emboldened by their reaction, the Gnasher slid its hand over her chest, curling its fingers above the frantic beating of her heart. It smiled a malicious smile.

"Goodbye, little songbird," it said, and thrust its hand deep inside her.

Cold flooded Penelope, chilling her down to the marrow in her bones. Goosebumps flared across her skin, but she felt little else, nothing close to pain. She stared at the Gnasher with confusion, the hand she'd crammed into her mouth barely holding place.

"You should be dead," the Gnasher said, eyes stricken. It yanked its hand free of her and threw a befuddled look at the others. "She should be dead!"

All eyes locked upon Penelope.

Penelope shuddered.

She bit into her hand, but the strain became too great for her to hold back any longer. The song burst from her mouth with the raw power of a hurricane, launching the Intruders in the air and through the walls and ceiling. Penelope scrambled to the window. She gathered them into her line of sight—each one dazed or thrashing as they thumped against the backyard lawn—and unleashed the song again.

Some crumbled into dust. Some rattled and shattered like resonated glass. Blisters devoured the Gnasher's skin before its flesh sloughed, and its bones collapsed into a heap of broken fragments. But Penelope didn't stop. She meant it to hurt, meant to keep them away for good, to encircle the neighborhood with a protective wall of sound. While her song echoed into the night, a few lights spilled from her neighbors' windows. Silhouettes draped upon their shades and curtains and she placed a hand against her window screen.

"Oh my God, shut up!"

"Seriously, this has gone on too long."

"Go. Away."

Penelope snatched her hand away. The song faded from her throat, leaving a swollen ache in its place. She lifted two fingers to the blood pooling on her cheek, but instead of wiping it she pressed it hard into her face. Her neighbors, they didn't understand. And that hurt her worse than any wound the Gnasher could have inflicted.

* * *

True to Old Woman's warning, Boss Man acted swiftly. Old Woman and Brown-Haired Girl helped Penelope pack her things into two boxes big enough for her meager wardrobe and an assortment of odds and ends. They led Penelope through the hallway—backed by the looming presence of Mean—past the rec room, past the dining room, and past the eyes of her oblivious housemates.

Penelope began to cry.

"It's not so bad," said Old Woman. "Your new place is nice. It's just...isolated. It'll be more peaceful, if you ask me. With no more blather or music playing at ungodly hours of the night, you might finally get a good night's rest. You'll see. You'll love it there."

"And that's where I work for most of the week, so you and I will have a chance to visit each other more often," said Brown-

Haired Girl.

When they reached the entryway, Penelope turned to face the long stretch of the banishment corridor. She pushed her gaze through the sliding glass door, beyond the men fixing the torn-up remnants of the backyard lawn and fence, to her neighbors' homes. One last look and never again.

From the corner of the rec room, Franklin popped his head into view, grinning with careless joy. He waved with more than just his hand; his whole body shook from the effort. It dawned on Penelope: this was worse than just the loss of another home, another place of belonging. When she left, everyone else would be defenseless.

She threw her teddy bear aside and ran to Franklin, struggling to balance her unsteady footfalls.

"Oh Lord, we got a runner," said Old Woman.

"I'll get her," said Brown-Haired Girl, dropping the box she held.

Once Penelope stood before Franklin, she stared into his eyes, picturing Intruders and forcing understanding into his mind. She motioned to the back yard and the black line of the horizon far beyond. He turned in that direction and she kissed him on the cheek, her lips tingling on his skin. Why and to what effect, she hadn't a clue, but she had to believe whatever had given her the power to fight Intruders had now been shared with Franklin.

Franklin touched his cheek with his fingertips and waved goodbye as Brown-Haired Girl steered Penelope down the hallway. Mean yanked the front door open, muttering words Penelope didn't bother hearing. For a moment, she could almost see her parents standing on the porch, still grieving, yet still unrelenting in their decision.

The last time she saw them she'd cried, but now she fixed them with a steely gaze, remembering all the things she'd done in just this week alone. She wasn't helpless; she never had been. Like her neighbors, they just didn't understand. With that, she strode through the door, dispelling their apparitions, and into the light of another solemn morning.

SO PRAISE HIM

MR. TODD STOOD POISED over the paraffin candles on the altar, thumb upon the flint wheel of his Zippo lighter. To his right, Pastor Stromm held his arms out, shaking as if he were supporting some enormous weight. All around the sanctuary, the congregation lifted one or both hands, eyes shut as they focused on that single word of invitation, "Come!"

That evening, on Pastor Stromm's insistence, we used a new approach to praise and worship, loud and ostentatious, like carnival barkers enticing passersby. He said he'd been researching the practice for years before bringing it to our attention and that it was the key to our success. But so far it'd been four nights of raucous praise and prayer, met by an apathetic silence from above and our own discontent. Despite it all, we pressed on.

"So praise Him," Pastor Stromm shouted, attempting to stir us into deeper supplication. "I can sense some of you are holding back. He wants to hear you, so praise Him!"

Voices lifted in a wall of sound. I tried again to join them. I closed my eyes, put my attention on that spot behind my eyelids where red and black swirled in an endless corridor of concentration. After another earnest attempt, I sighed and leaned back into my seat.

Guilt tugged at the muscles of my gut. No matter how much I wanted to participate, Pastor Stromm was right: something did hold me back. Perhaps nerves. Perhaps confusion. But mostly fear that our desperate cries for attention were no better than a pack of noisy dogs, barking and scuffling up the trunk of the wrong tree.

* * *

At the beginning of the fifth day's service, disappointment ran high. Though I chose to remain quietly indignant, the grumbling from others in the parish came in a widespread baritone murmur. Pastor Stromm reacted quickly. He raised a hand and everyone fell silent.

"I can sense the doubt among you, but you *must* hold steadfast if you wish to reap the benefits."

He put his hands behind his back, began pacing the stage with eyes downcast. Equal parts Charlie Chaplin shuffle and a death row march to the electric chair.

"You've heard me mention this story already, shared with me by the great granddaughter of the man, Francis Seymour, himself. In 1850, the Ten Faithful of Vinewood Street met in Pastor Seymour's house to collect in prayer. It was a humble house, not much more than dust and hardwood flooring. Hardly a temple fit for God. I dare say, for five weeks, nothing happened beyond good old-fashioned fellowship and a whole lot of *sore knees*."

On cue, a chuckle from the crowd.

"But on the sixth week, the last day of a planned three-day fast"—he slammed a palm against the pulpit, with a wood shivering crash—"the Divine Presence shook up that house and everyone inside it. *Changed* them somehow, once and forever."

His theatrics did their job. The congregation responded with an enthusiastic, "Amen!" that had them shifting in their seats.

"Now, Seymour's wife left the group soon after and took their daughter with her. She lacked the faith, lacked the conviction, to carry on. Both wife and daughter lost out on the blessings poured out from that day forward, something I gather they both regretted until their dying days. But *this* close to the finish line, we can't be guilty of the same, can we?"

He fell still, turned toward the audience and dropped his arms into a loose shrug.

"Of course not... So praise Him!"

The response was instantaneous. Our voices lifted in accord and hands shot up so fast one might have thought Pastor Stromm had threatened to dive into the crowd. Soon, the sanctuary filled to bursting with hopeful cries and singing. Everywhere, people began to shake in turns, as if a low electric current progressed from person to person and pew to pew. Pastor Stromm dropped to his knees. Mr. Todd rested his chin on his palms and his elbows on the altar. He lit his face with a closed-eyed smile, having quite forgotten the ritual lighting of the candles.

Even I wasn't immune. I could feel heat gathering in my chest and in my palms. A buzzing started in my brain and the world teetered like an ocean. For a moment, I was a raft thrown about by violent, cresting waves, which threatened to swallow me up in their vast waters. I choked, if only on the idea. But then I realized the sensation wasn't breathlessness, rather strange words attempting to rise unbidden from my throat.

"*Kamsssa isss-cryp sssak-reepee—*"

The spell soon broke when Anthony, the Leftkes' boy, turned around and stared. Amid the maelstrom of similar gibberish shouted by the other parishioners, I could feel his gaze—those twin beams of absent-mindedness—burrowing into my skin. When our eyes met, he shoved a finger into his nostril and dug around. It didn't come out alone, and I couldn't bear the thought or sight of it drifting to his open, waiting mouth. I hurried from the sanctuary to stem the rising tide of sick.

Once I stepped into the night, I took in a deep breath. The light of the only working lamppost wavered from half a block away and then fizzled out. After that, the street teemed with a dark and eerie silence, transforming trees into giants caught in a ceremonial sway, cars into crouching beasts waiting for unsuspecting passersby.

Once my stomach settled, I focused on the waning moon, let my eyes absorb its soft trim of glowing blue. We were a church of the Calvinist tradition and, for the most part, held ourselves proper and restrained. Though we were open to outward shows of worship, they were never anything on this level. And never before had there been such a demonstrative response to our efforts. Whatever it was, it'd brought more than just mesmerizing warmth, disorientation, and the compulsion to make strange noises. There was hunger in it—a need stronger than the pulse of our collective desire, maybe even stronger than our will.

I didn't bother going back inside.

* * *

On the sixth day, I almost didn't attend the service. The experience from the previous night left a hollow ache inside me, as if I were a battery drained of all its juice. It wasn't so much physical weariness, but as if some indistinct quality deep within me had been ripped loose.

Nevertheless, my sense of obligation was the stronger pull. I'd been attending the church for nine years, had grown fond of many of its members. We may not have been blood, but we were family even so. It was a small congregation by most accounts, only fifty strong, including children. No matter what I believed had happened, it seemed wrong to leave them now.

I arrived a few minutes late. The left of the heavy double-doors groaned shut as I crept inside the sanctuary, offering an apologetic nod to the curious, and a guilty smile and shrug to the withering looks tossed my way. Pastor Stromm had already started the first of many micro-sermons to kick off the service, so I took the first empty seat in the rear-most pew.

"It'll be a *hundred and fifty years*, tomorrow, since the Ten Faithful left Shelton behind for good, to preach the Good News throughout the world. From the testimony of the great granddaughter, power and signs preceded them, the likes of which mankind had never seen before. That could be *us*. We're on the brink of something truly extraordinary tonight."

We all clapped, though mine seemed by far the less enthusiastic.

"Tonight, we claim our heritage by walking the same path set out for us by our spiritual ancestors. Storming the gates, as it were, until God can't *help* but answer our call—can I get an amen?"

"Amen!"

"So praise Him!"

It started simple, same as the previous nights. But then the presence returned and it became different, progressed into something...wrong. I opened my eyes, took a look around the sanctuary. The strips of halogen above us winked out and Mr. Todd lit the candles one by one. The stained-glass windows behind the pulpit—brightened by the setting sun—sparkled like jewels, bathing us in beams of primary light. All around me voices rose, low and throaty, high and tinkling, laughing, sobbing, and some even screaming babble.

I could feel it trying to force its way inside me—a sensation like warm water blasting from a nozzle. Only it was everywhere, all at once, and not even clothes or skin could hold it at bay.

"Stop," I said, as it poured through hidden channels into the reservoir of my soul. My tongue lolled in my mouth and I bit the tip hard when the word "*kamsssa*" slithered from my throat. At the same time, I grabbed my arms, pressed myself against the backrest to keep my body from thrashing.

It wasn't hard to guess the presence was doing the same to others. I heard a growl to my right. Kathy, the Sunday school teacher, dropped on all fours and proceeded to galumph along the center aisle, growling and barking in turns. Martin and Cynthia, a newlywed couple, began to laugh harder and harder, until they collapsed in their seats, gasping for air. Some roared like lions, others fell prostrate to the floor, and others still convulsed as if caught in seizures.

"Stop this," I yelled to Pastor Stromm. "It's gone too far!"

He didn't hear me. He tore at his clothes, screaming, "I'm burning with the glory, burning with the glory!" with tears sliding down his cheeks.

"This isn't right," I called behind me, struggling for the exit.

On my way out, I spotted Anthony, eyes streaming tears, nose streaming worse. All of the other children I saw cried too, but unlike Pastor Stromm, it wasn't rapture on their faces. They stared up at the ecstatic displays in helpless terror, searching the faces of their parents for relief, but finding only chaos.

* * *

For the seventh day, Pastor Stromm booked Mount Adahy, a conference center located in a backwoods southeast of San Gabriel. We'd held our yearly church getaway there for the last five years, so it was familiar ground. Beyond the complex proper, dirt paths twisted through forested terrain, choked by conifers, oaks, maples, laurels, and a dozen other species besides. Less than a mile north from the sanctuary, the Pontayo River marked the border of the property. And all around, the sanctity of nature: air fresh as new creation, drenched in birdsong and the moldering scent of litterfall.

Shame that it would be wasted on a thing like this.

The afternoon and early evening had been set aside for free time, family events, and dinner. I arrived late, during the hour of preparation for the evening service. When I entered the conference sanctuary, I found Pastor Stromm's wife seated on the front row pew, lilting her head and singing a hymn about a fountain of blood and the sinners who plunged inside it. Mr. Todd fixed up a makeshift altar out of a folding table and a tablecloth on which to set the candlesticks. As for Pastor Stromm, he paced the stage, muttering things I couldn't hear over the distance.

Once he saw me, he waved and smiled, causing his white and gray speckled mustache to lift into a lazy M.

"Ah, an eager beaver! Welcome, Wesley. We saved you a spot up front," he said, with a mischievous wink.

I hurried over, greeted Mr. Todd and Mrs. Stromm with a nod along the way, and said to the pastor behind a cupped hand, "Do you have time to talk?"

"Of course," said Pastor Stromm.

"In private?"

"If necessary."

We headed through a side door to outside. Most of the congregation remained in the dining hall. However, Mr. and Mrs. Bettridge strolled the complex, their kids chasing after chattering squirrels, and Martin and Cynthia, the laughing couple, sat on a wooden bench as they gazed—thoughtful and composed—into the foliage above. All appeared calm and, I must admit, it shook my convictions over what I'd come to say.

"Pastor Stromm, I'm worried about tonight's service."

"Whatever for?"

"I have my doubts about all this, for lack of a better term, strangeness. It has the feel of menace, not the peace you'd expect from something good. Beyond that..." I glanced around to ensure we weren't being overheard, and seeing we were not, I whispered in a conspiratorial tone. "The way people lost control and the chaos that ensued the last few nights? If it happens again, someone might get hurt."

He folded his arms. "Yes, I admit things have gotten a bit hectic. Tonight will be different, though. You'll see."

"I don't know, Pastor Stromm." There was so much more I couldn't say, feelings and intuitions that had stirred my concern, but resisted all attempts at explanation. "Maybe we'd be better off canceling the whole thing."

"I can't do that. After all our hard work, how can I tell them it was for nothing?"

"Do what you believe is right. However, I'm not sure I can take part anymore."

His eyes narrowed and his cheeks drew up tight. "Wesley, you

* * *

Closer to the complex, before the trees thinned out completely, I ducked into a thicket and searched for movement. The power had been cut, and the only light came from emergency back-up lamps—one or two tucked into the corners of every building. Far from easing my fear, it made it worse. Enough light persisted to accentuate the black pools of shadow, expanding and contracting like living, breathing things.

I cast a glance into the deep of the forest. In the direction of the river, I could hear manic laughter, similar in kind to the sixth-day service, only coarser and utterly mirthless. Interspersed among it was the sound of coughing, sputtering, terrified shrieks. And then more laughter.

After a few more moments, I braved the open space, creeping forward in long, quiet strides. When I stepped into the path between the dining hall and the nursery, the darkness ahead of me clarified into a figure. It was Anthony, the Leftke boy, standing alone in the middle of the walkway.

"Anthony," I whispered. "Are you alone? Where are your parents?"

He didn't speak, didn't move. If anything, he held more still.

I crept closer. The second I could see the details of his face—his empty eyes and the thin line of his mouth—he lifted a finger and plunged it into his nostril. It didn't stop. The wet sound of sliding gave way to a hollow crack and the nostril split from the fat of his knuckle. When he finally pulled it out again, something big, red, and meaty clung to its tip.

"Oh dear God," I said, and he sneered at my words, lipping the chunk and pulling the finger away clean.

I ran past, giving him a wide berth. Within moments, I tripped over something soft lying across the walkway. It was Martin and Cynthia, and they were dead. Their eyes bulged from their sockets, mouths stretched out in cheek-splitting grins, baring every tooth. Their skin was tinted a shade that could have been gray or blue, as if they'd choked on their own laughter.

There was no time to react. A series of growls alerted me of something prowling in the far-off bushes, and just around the building. Perhaps humans emulating animals, but nothing like the embarrassing display of the sixth-day sermon when Kathy scampered down the aisle on hands and knees. These were unrestrained, violent, and debased articulations—the sound of madness—and they were converging on me.

I backtracked toward the forest, but more growls came from that direction, so I turned again, retreated down the walkway that skirted past the sanctuary. There, beside the entrance, Mr. Todd stood behind the makeshift altar. The sight of him flooded me with relief—until I noticed what he was doing. In place of the candles lay three severed heads, hair slicked up in even spires. Mr. Todd studied the closest one, flicked his Zippo, and put the flame against its tip. Each time, the spire sizzled and smoked, but never stayed lit. That didn't stop him from trying again and again.

"What is this?" I said.

He looked up in surprise, as if he'd only just noticed me.

"Ah, Wesley. There you are," he said, his voice soft, even gentle. "Pastor Stromm is looking for you. He said to say, if I should come upon you, that he'd failed to live up to his promise, and that if it were any consolation, he now admits you were right and had every reason to worry."

"Pastor...Stromm?"

"Yes. If you want to speak to him, you'll have to step inside," he said, motioning to the sanctuary door.

More murderous growls, this time from every direction.

"Better hurry. The hounds are drawing near," he said. "And just between you and me, I think a few of them are angry you missed the doling out of holy gifts."

I nodded, though I don't know why, and ducked through the doorway. The wall-mounted emergency lamps inside were drenched with blood, bathing the sanctuary in the crimson light of a darkroom. A dozen bodies lay slumped against the pews, a few poised as if sleeping, others ripped apart and scattered along the aisles. Pastor Stromm stood on the stage, his arms held out and wavering from an invisible weight—just like during the fourth-day sermon. Only now, they were stumps, severed just above the elbow joint.

"What happened? What did this to you?" I asked, my hands clenched and held out on both sides, to steady myself while passing through the slicks of blood.

He turned his head, nothing else, in my direction. "Oh, Wesley. You're still here? I'd hoped you had escaped all this."

"Where is everyone?"

"Most of them are by the river. Drowning the children and then themselves. I'm sure you heard the rest skulking about outside."

"The Ten Faithful. They never served on any worldwide mission, did they? They got the attention of the other side all right, but it wasn't Heaven. It was Hell."

"Hmmm, yes, I may have been a bit hasty in my conclusions. The evidence was circumstantial at best, but I thought I had it right. In any case, nothing good came of the Ten Faithful of Vinewood, of that we can be certain," he said, stretching his stumps to indicate the state of the sanctuary. "But you're wrong about the latter part."

"What do you mean?"

"It wasn't Hell unleashed tonight. In fact, I suspect things are a *lot* more complicated than we had ever imagined."

He nudged his face forward, indicating something behind me.

I turned and saw a man wearing nothing but a loincloth standing in the doorway, his skin spoiled by deep gouges dripping rivulets of blood. "Come," he said, his voice strong, but nondescript. Everyone's voice, but no one's voice. "You've earned your rest."

He took a step, stretching out his arms as if intending to embrace me, revealing holes punched into his wrists. I spun around to face Pastor Stromm, my mind screaming babble from a madness I hadn't yet succumbed to. I couldn't find the words I needed, so I aimed my agony, my grief, my disbelief—everything left within me—in Pastor Stromm's direction.

He nodded. "We called and He came."

Fingers curled around my shoulder, bearing the same weight and pressure as that familiar presence. Though the hand remained solid, something entered me. My insides shuddered; that indefinable energy began to drain away. Then my mind unfolded, and the universe revealed itself—the false dichotomy of things I took for granted: darkness and light, heat and cold, being and nothingness, sanity and madness, good and evil. Mere forms of the same existence. Different modes of the same underlying power, all bearing the same substance.

And all of it derived from Him.

I fell to the ground, staring up at the presence now made manifest as it loomed above me, face etched with both eternal indifference and endless compassion.

"So praise Him," said Pastor Stromm, before a void of laughter consumed us both.

* * *

A day or so passed in a forgetful blur. When something like reason returned to me again, I found Mrs. Stromm alive. She told me she'd stepped out to the bathroom shortly after she delivered the seventh-day announcements, and when she heard the tumult, she locked the doors and hid inside a stall. Together, we searched for other survivors, but found no one, no bodies, not even blood. All signs of violence had been wiped away, as had the personal effects and property of the dead or missing members of our church. As far as it appeared, they never came.

After that, we parted company and headed back to Shelton. For months, we were questioned about the disappearances by authorities, journalists, and the families of the congregation. Without collusion, Mrs. Stromm and I answered them in the same way, the only way we could: with truth.

By the will of God, they left this world behind.

THE LAST GREAT FAILING OF THE LIGHT

SOLIS HAD COMMENCED AND the Festival of the Forever Sun was well underway. Ever since dawn's first light peered over the horizon, townspeople crammed the streets of Magtagal in honor of longer days and shorter nights. Even children joined the gaiety, laughing and chanting as they waved their golden streamers through the air.

As for me, I had no time for drinking and dancing, for the singing of raucous songs, for food carts and trinket sellers, or for the evening feasts in the dining hall, where they wheeled in roasted hogs with their throats slit and their insides hollowed out. Since I'd been born in distant lands, Solis days meant little more to me than extra light to bleed, and sweat, and toil.

I woke early with all the others, but spent the brunt of the morning peeling wood from my neighbor Amado's rooftop. By noon, I managed to isolate the damage he'd long suspected. It was a patch of dry rot three meters long and half as wide, a simple fix even with the few tools I'd brought. But as I began to carve away the feeble timber from the rafters, sunlight began to waver and an airy roar melded with the sound of rushing winds. Clouds appeared, thick and black as smoke. They sailed across the vault of heaven, and once they reached the opposite horizon, day descended into dusk.

"Is it a storm?" a young girl asked, tugging on her father's arm.

Fear gripped me. I clasped my hands to steady their tremble, even as I turned to address the crowd below. "No, this is worse. This is dayglow!"

The townspeople drew together for comfort. Some gasped, some shook, some turned away. Most stared on in confusion, having been born too late to remember the Great Failing of the Light, a time that nearly brought humanity to extinction.

"It means the Kivranmak has awoken," I continued. "The Iblis have returned. We must flee before it's too late!"

This everyone understood, and panic swept the streets.

* * *

The Kivranmak—a giant ball of many eyes and tangled flesh—tumbled through the sky like a moon let loose from the firmament. A horde of Ibli monstrosities swarmed across the western scrublands, and in the ocean to the north. While some townspeople waited for the Datu's orders, the rest of us hurried to our homes to prepare for evacuation.

It didn't take long for me to assemble provisions. I loaded two packs with blankets, clothes, food and water, and a barrow full of wood for fires. No sooner had I opened my door than the crier's voice rang out, backed by the steady thump of men on horseback.

"By the Datu's decree, every male must arm themselves and gather by the shoreline."

My heart shuddered as I stowed my things away, and went to greet Bayani, the leader of the maharlika. He and over fifty of his men were organizing the assembly, already wearing the deep red baros of their battle dress. Men waved to their wives and daughters, boys to their mothers and sisters, their faces grim or soaked in tears as they lined up, single file.

"Be reasonable, Bayani," I said. "If all the remaining powers of the world united, we still couldn't defeat the Iblis. Let us leave. If the Datu wants to save this town, he and his family can stay behind and guard it."

Bayani cantered closer and regarded me with tightly knitted brows. "We have our orders, Marden, and so do you."

I leaned in close, lowered my voice. "Then consider I'm not from here. I have no roots, no wife or children. For years, I've labored for the good of Magtagal, but in the end I fight and die for no one."

He glowered and tossed me a sword, still in its scabbard. I caught it and hefted its foreign weight in my hands.

"Coward. You've enjoyed our town in times of peace, now defend it in our time of war," he said.

"There won't be any war today, just our extermination."

Bayani nodded, his expression resolute, as if he already knew the truth of it.

* * *

We stood four hundred strong when all were accounted for. At the farthest edges of our perimeter, we lit bonfires, a measure known to ward off smaller Iblis. Five heavy cannons were spread out to face each advancing front. Behind them loomed the maharlika on horseback, armed with swords and flintlock rifles. The rest of us—fishers, metalsmiths, weavers, merchants, servants, carpenters, and farmers—crowded in the rear. With weapons drawn and brandished, we stared in fear and awe as the Ibli horde drew closer.

The Kivranmak arrived first. Once it settled over Magtagal, a hush fell and every face turned toward that quivering mass of flesh. Far from a mindless brute, a look of cunning filled the many eyes strewn across its body. Each of them returned our stares as if probing, counting, determining our fate. Silence gave way to a rumble of terror that spread throughout our ranks; I used the confusion to steal away.

After collecting the provisions from my house, I slipped back into the streets. A faint wind ruffled golden streamers, their tail ends slithering in the dust, supple and alive. Cries from wives and daughters leaked through the walls of their hiding places, and I imagined them as bleating goats awaiting the coming slaughter. Once I reached the edge of town, I strode into the plains beyond the southern border.

"Marden!" a voice shouted from behind me.

Malea stood buried in the shadow of the Kivranmak, an arm wrapped around her son, Lawin. I'd known her for many years: a wash maid during working hours, but something more to the rich merchant Danilo at night. She'd always been a frail thing, but with the blackness of her hair framing the borders of her sallow face, she looked almost cadaverous.

"Go home and hide, Malea. It isn't safe out here."

"Take us with you," she said, dropping to her knees, forcing her son down next to her. "Please!"

"You may come," I said at once—a moment of pity, a weakness—cursing the words as soon as they passed from my lips.

A blur of motion on the outskirts of town caught my eye, as if something had risen from the ground and bounded in Malea's direction. However, when my eyes settled on the spot, I found nothing but dust and empty shadows. We ran from that place with all our might. Shouts grew and merged with the sporadic crack of gunfire, and the tremulous booms of cannons. But soon, the Iblis' wicked howls absorbed all sound, save for the chorus of screams that followed.

* * *

Three miles south we turned to gauge our progress. Before, the Kivranmak swung in patient arcs; now its body made violent rotations, as if spurring on its horde. Directly beneath it, Magtagal lay wrapped in squirming darkness, everything from the houses lining its borders to the tip of the central temple's steeple. Forty years had passed since I'd seen a sight like this, but I felt no different than I had then. My body shook, and my insides screamed until all that was left inside me was a hollow ache.

"Are we safe now?" asked Lawin.

"Yes, we're safe," said Malea, hugging him close, wiping the tears from his eyes.

"Do you promise?"

"I promise. Nothing can hurt us now."

If I could have peeled my eyes away, I might have shouted at her for the harm she'd done, the false hope she had imparted. Fleeting comfort was no excuse for reckless words. While our hunger for life had impelled us toward the mere chance of refuge, in truth there was no safety—save for those buried six feet under, who had no cares or worries left.

* * *

We continued on for some time. Lawin's child legs slowed us to a plod, and Malea was no better, stooped under the weight of a single pack. By the time we stopped for rest, we'd only added another four miles between us and the memory of home.

We camped in the barrens, spotted by clumps of withered grass left over from the rain season. I'd heard it had once been a thriving route between cities, where merchants lugged their wares to and from every corner of the continent. But trade had dried up along with the Great Failing of the Light, leaving it abandoned—except for wagon tracks pressed into the earth like remnants of an ancient civilization.

I set up a warding fire while Malea and Lawin laid out our bedding. They drifted off soon after, leaving me to keep watch alone. A curtain of night descended around us. Earlier, I'd seen a ridge of hills to the west, and to the east a grove of mahogany, withered and charnel. Now the world bled black too thick for human eyes to pierce.

In the silence, I thought about the movement I'd seen in the shadows before we'd left Magtagal. So much more threatening now that I was in a calmer state of mind. Briefly, I wondered if we'd been followed, if even now the Iblis were converging on our position, ready to burst into our midst and finish what they'd started. Though it may have been a product of my idling brain, I couldn't shake the feeling that the darkness gathered in, watching us, and waiting.

* * *

The next day we woke and assembled our gear. Dayglow remained, reducing the sun to a faint crimson ball. To the north, the Kivranmak hung above Magtagal, throbbing like a beating heart. It could only mean one thing: the town had been destroyed, its people butchered. Malea wept in swells when she saw it, and Lawin—too young to interpret the tidings of that sky behemoth—held her hand against his cheek.

"Don't cry, Mommy. We're safe, remember? You promised me we're safe."

Despite myself, I laughed. Somewhere far off I thought I heard the laughter caught up and echoed by another voice. Baleful, deeper toned, quiet so that it filled only the narrow cracks of silence.

"Let's go," I said, eager to press on.

We swung east to collect more firewood. Up close, the mahogany grove appeared no larger than a lake, with trees spread wide as if each preferred their solitude among the collective. Focused in the center clearing, bones lay jumbled among the dust and litterfall, laced with the fragments of wagon tarps. No doubt the vestige of some previous Ibli awakening.

"You two stay here," I said and rolled the barrow in.

I collected fallen twigs for kindling and tore branches off the brittle trees. Once I replaced what we'd used the previous night, I hurried out—noticing movement only when I'd rounded on the barrens. A horse skull was seated on a pile of bones, its lower jaw hanging wide, its blackened sockets fixed on me. I took another step to test my suspicions and, sure enough, it swiveled and caught me again within its line of sight. It had to be an Ibli, and now it had my measure.

"I see you," I said, pulling my sword from its scabbard.

"I see you," it repeated, its voice coarse, flapping the horse's lower jaw as if to mock me.

The skull's sockets wept gray and its mouth vomited the same. The runoff collected in a pile and hardened like a scab. Compound eyes emerged across its body. Tentacles bloomed from its torso and a beak extended like a spear from the center of its face. I barely had time to lift my sword before it was upon me.

It flailed its appendages like whips, darting away from the inelegant swing of my blade. I managed to sever a plot of eyes, but the wound mended before it even bled. I wasn't so lucky. Blood streamed from the gashes it slapped into my arms and side, making my hands slick and wet, weakening my grip. After it ensnared my leg, I fell to my knees. It wasted no time surging forward, stabbing me in the chest with its beak, thrashing its body side to side to force itself in deeper.

To my surprise, I felt no pain. My mind drifted to better days, long before the word "Ibli" held meaning. Back to a particular night when my parents had put me to bed at the end of a blazing Solis day. "You're safe. We'll always protect you," they'd said, as earnest and false as Malea's promise to Lawin. With that, I collapsed to the ground, lost in a roiling cloud of numbness.

* * *

"Martin? Martin, what's wrong?" Malea said, standing beside me with a hand upon my shoulder.

Her clothes had changed, no longer the mishmash brown and white stripes of a peasant. Now she wore a clean silk baro and matching skirt, swirling with shades of yellow, the color of—

"Sunlight," I said.

I looked up. Tucked into a corner of the sky, the sun burned fierce and unrestrained. I reached a hand out toward its warmth, laughing, clapping, chanting, "Dayglow is through! They've gone to sleep! The Iblis have gone to sleep!"

Malea stepped back. She folded her arms, unsure, as if I were the fool who didn't understand.

"Malea, don't you know what this means?" I said.

"It's *Maleha*," she said, cocking her head. "Martin, you're acting so strange."

"Marden," I said in the same admonishing tone she'd used.

As quickly as I spoke, I knew I was mistaken. In that moment I became aware of this new world, with sprawling cities that spanned the continents—the kind of civilization that could only arise if the Iblis never were. My whole life flashed before me. The enduring peace of it. The simplicity that came without the constant threat of death. But more than that, I saw my time with Maleha: our courtship, our wedding, the birth of our son Heath, who was different from Lawin in that his eyes were green, not brown. Here, I hadn't merely endured; I'd lived and loved, and even made a family.

I shuddered, not from fear this time, but because of the intoxicating joy I felt. Despite the terrors of the night before, blessed daylight had ret—

* * *

Dried old mahogany. Stunted dayglow. Staring at the desiccated earth level with my eyes.

"No," I said, pushing myself from the ground, wishing I could rip the unwelcome sight away like a veil from my eyes.

From what I'd gathered since the Great Failing of the Light, there were two kinds of Iblis: those that devoured flesh, and those that consumed the minds of men. When the Kivranmak came for the city of my birth, my parents hid me beneath the floorboards of our house. I watched through cracks as the Iblis ravaged them and ate them piece by piece. Besides me, two others had survived that day. Whatever they'd seen had driven them beyond insanity, to a place where self-harm was their only source of comfort. Since I was alive, it wasn't hard to guess which kind of Ibli I'd just met.

"Where did it go?" I asked, my voice croaking.

"Gone," said Malea. "It grabbed your sword and slipped back into the grove."

"Are you injured? Where's Lawin?"

"He's fine. We're both fine. You're what matters now. We saw you fall and believed that you were—"

"Not yet."

Shifting to a seated position, I lifted my baro to inspect my wound, bracing for the worst. But no puncture, not even a scar, marred the skin of my chest. The sigh that escaped my mouth would have made the winds blush with envy. After Malea bound my arms and leg with strips from her skirt, we headed south again, fully stocked with wood.

Most of my life I'd walked in silence, my mind left open to impressions made by my surroundings. This time I tried to forget that hallucination, or dream, or whatever it may have been. Yet try as I might, I could still feel the warmth of sunlight and knew that for a moment, for one perfect stretch of time, I'd found true happiness.

* * *

Five miles onward, the barrens gave way to a meadow dotted with orange poppies and the occasional oak. The range of hills I'd seen before formed a barrier to our right. From our vantage point, I couldn't tell how deep they ran, and with the way I'd been favoring my right leg, I hoped we'd never have to find out.

We rested under a thriving mango tree. There we ate more than salted meats and dried rice. Malea and I were ambivalent for the reprieve, but Lawin munched his share of mango like a special treat.

"Do you like them?" I said to Lawin, offering him another.

He looked at me, stunned, and took it from my hand without a word. I returned his stare with a flushed sort of confusion. After all, I'd never spoken to him before, nor had I ever wanted to. So why had I started now?

From then on, no one said a word, save for Lawin's happy chatter as he lay and poked insects on the ground. Malea took out a comb and began unraveling the tangles of her hair. As for me, that other place still dominated my thoughts. The years of Martin's life remained stark and fresh within my mind, as if they were true memories.

A side glance from Malea before she asked, "What's wrong? Are your wounds still bothering you?"

"No, just thinking."

"About that Ibli that attacked you?"

"Not exactly."

"Then what?"

I almost huffed and turned away like I'd done to her so many times before, both on this journey and during our various encounters in Magtagal. But when I looked into her eyes, the mirror reflection of Maleha—save for her slumped posture, and a look of perpetual despair— the anger didn't come.

"Do you believe in other worlds?"

She winced. "You mean the afterlife? Like paradise and punishment, the realm of Eternal Day or world of Endless Night? Feels like we're already living in the latter."

"I mean something much like this one, but for a single difference. Like a place where the sun is blue or the grass is red. Or a place where the Iblis never existed."

She smiled, but it quickly slid into a frown. "No. Do you?"

"Would it be so strange if I did?"

She chewed the words inside her mind, and then said, "Yes. It sounds much too hopeful, and you, Marden, have never struck me as a hopeful man."

* * *

Sometime before nightfall, the Kivranmak drifted over us, its motion punctuated by sporadic jerks. Already we could hear the Iblis, their ecstatic moans lacing the wind, low as the rumble before an earthquake. We turned east, entering a broad dale, and managed to bed down before the hidden sun slipped below the horizon.

Before I settled in, I scanned the borders of our camp. For a second, I thought I saw a few pinpoints of light beyond the fire's range, and imagined the Ibli from before, its compound eyes glaring through the darkness.

"I see you," I said.

There came no response, but I had every intention of keeping the fire strong until dayglow returned. I lay down, facing stars that would not twinkle and a moon that would not shine, pretending Maleha was by my—

* * *

I returned to that sunlit world, now standing in a garden behind a house I knew was mine. Malkohas clicked and warbled from the branches of the surrounding trees. Across the way, a white cat skirted the edges of a trunk, measuring the distance between itself and the lowest branches. What's more, the air tasted fresh, bearing the sweet scent of plumeria, and the grass felt thick and soft beneath my bare feet. While I knew this had to be a dream, nothing in it struck me as false.

A familiar voice said, "Are you sure you're all right? You've been acting strange for days now."

I spun around and found Maleha, her expression pinched and worried. "Yes. I'm fine."

A flutter filled my chest and I swallowed deep to loosen the lump building in my throat. Then I remembered that, here, I was Martin and Maleha was my wife. The nervousness I felt melted away at once and I embraced her, taking in her warmth, her scent, the feel of her body pressing into mine.

"What are you doing?" she said, sweeping glances all around. "Someone may see us."

"There's nothing wrong with a husband holding his wife."

She laughed and my insides stirred. "But in public? Some might call it unseemly."

"Let *some* call it what they like. I doubt I have much time left, and I don't want to waste it worrying about the opinions of prying neighbors—I had a thought. You and me and Heath should have a picnic. We'll go to the beach, enjoy the sun—"

She eased herself from my grip. "Can't. I have errands to run, and Heath is coming with me. In fact, I'm late already. I only came to check on you, but I really should be going." She lifted up on tiptoes to kiss my cheek. "Love you, Martin."

"I love you, too," I said, and I realized I meant it.

* * *

I wasn't surprised when I woke lying in a bed of grass, but the frantic scream that had roused me from my sleep struck me senseless. Malea was huddled next to Lawin, crushing him in her grip, rocking back and forth, his name pouring from her throat in shrieks and wails. I didn't have to see him for myself to know that he was dead.

I threw myself beside Malea, wanting to console her, wanting to hold her like I'd held Maleha only moments before. But I couldn't. When I saw the state of Lawin's body, it took all my strength to twist away and keep myself from vomiting.

Lawin. He could have been my son, but for the Iblis. Could have been my friend but for the hate inside me, born of four decades' worth of misery. I'd treated him like nothing—nothing—and now I could never make it right.

"Show yourself!" I yelled between cupped hands, rising to my feet and glaring into the distance.

There came no response, no sound, except the gentle hiss of wind blowing through the tall grass. As I staggered back to Malea, the echo of laughter from days before returned, still baleful, still low, hidden in the cover of silence like a shadow in the dark. We tarried in that place for hours. Malea huddled over Lawin while I dug a burial hole. I started by using the flat end of a branch to break the ground, but in the end, it proved easier to use my hands. Besides, the dirt and stones that wedged between my fingers and nails felt comforting, a token sacrifice of pain to honor Lawin's memory.

We laid his body inside the groove I'd made—careful to assemble his parts into their proper place—and covered him. Malea smoothed out the rough edges of the mound before collapsing on top of it for one final, tearful goodbye.

"Any last words?" I said.

She looked up at me. "You spoke before about other worlds. I only hope they do exist, and that one day, somehow, I'll join Lawin there."

"I believe they do. One way or another, we'll both see him again."

She rose to her feet and hugged me, kissed my cheek several times before falling into my embrace. I kept silent, allowing the solace of the moment to linger.

We traveled on, but slower than before. My wounds had worsened, the red and swollen veins of infection creeping up my leg, reducing me to a hobble, and Malea went no faster in her grief. Before long, the darkness took us by surprise, forcing us to build our fire in a hurry. Once we set out our bedding, Malea rested her head upon my lap. I raked my fingers through her hair, humming ancient songs of comfort that my mother used to sing. Malea drifted off to sleep, still crying.

As I watched her slumber, it pained me to see how weary she looked—so frail a blade of grass might snap her bones. And yet, it didn't detract one ounce from her beauty. Now that Martin and I were one, in some way Maleha had also merged with Malea, and the feeling I had for this woman of soft snores and tear-stained cheeks surprised me with its suddenness and depth.

"My love," I whispered, and the words felt natural on my lips, as if a void had always been there, waiting for her to fill it.

Somewhere southwest of us, the guttural cries of the Iblis strengthened, too near for me to feel at ease. I wondered what town or city they ravaged now, or how many more would fall before their thirst for blood was quenched. But more so, I wondered how much time remained for Malea and me, two travelers on the open road to nowhere.

* * *

When daybreak came, we spotted the city of Karagatan arrayed beside the coast. Though distant, we savored the thought of their future hospitality and the hope of restoring our supplies. But during the early hours of our trek, the Kivranmak glided past us and settled above our destination. The Iblis couldn't be too far behind.

We quickened our pace, glancing around to discover the route the Iblis had taken. For a while, all seemed calm. I began to hope they'd been waylaid by the maharlika of some other city, long enough for us to make it through the dale. That hope didn't last for long. The Iblis' moans drifted in from the west, and we turned to find a swelling line of black devouring the landscape.

"What do we do?" said Malea, eyeing the Kivranmak and the Iblis in turn.

The dale hedged us in along the north and south with rampant hills too steep to climb. But farther east, I spotted the means of our escape.

"See there?" I said, pointing to where the northern ridge petered into hillocks.

"We'll never make it," said Malea, already panting.

"We have to try."

I shoved the barrow aside and ran, pushing through the pain, dragging Malea by the hand. When we fell, we helped each other up. When we stumbled, we pulled each other straight. Yet despite it all, the Ibli horde drew nearer.

By the end of the first mile, their cries intensified into roars. By the end of the second, their roars changed into a chorus of deafening screeches, and the black line of their advancing front broke into a herd of silhouettes. By the third mile, the Iblis clarified further. Most were humanoid, but others crept on all fours, and others still were undulating masses so twisted and twined within themselves they defied description.

Finally, my leg gave out and I collapsed, too heavy for Malea to lift me. Nevertheless, she tried and each time ended up on the ground beside me.

"It's no use," she said.

"No, it can't end like this."

"But—"

"It can't!"

I wouldn't give up, not with everything at stake: a life with someone I loved who might someday learn to love me, too. So long as I breathed, we would crawl to safety. And that's exactly what I did, inching along, dragging the hopeless Malea against her will. We gained ten more feet before the Ibli that had murdered Lawin pooled above the surface of the soil. It solidified, staring through its outcropped eyes, shifting to block our path in whatever direction we ventured.

"Let us pass!" I screamed.

The Ibli chuckled, that same baleful laughter I'd heard before. I realized that it had been following us from the beginning, that it may have even been the shadow I'd seen at Magtagal's border. For what purpose, to what end, I couldn't guess.

"You spared my life this long, so spare it again. What use will I be if I fall into the hands of your bloodthirsty kin?"

The Ibli sprouted tentacles, one on each side of its bulbous body. "Sleep," it said.

My body locked. I fell to my side and the world drained into a void.

* * *

I woke again in Martin's garden and crumbled to my knees, facing the sun, taking it in until my eyes burned and watered. I prayed to every power I could think of, every god or demon who had ever been said to concern themselves with the fleeting world of man.

"Malea," I said, clenching my fists so that my nails cut into my palms. "I'll come back for you."

My words rang false even to my ears. Nevertheless, I meant them and vowed to make them true. From then on I braced myself, trying not to think about what I would find when I returned.

* * *

When I opened my eyes, I looked around. Our packs had been shredded into fine strips of leather, and our supplies were crushed and scattered into the dust. A glance at Karagatan confirmed the Iblis had already passed me, but I couldn't find a sign of Malea. Not a scrap of clothes, a strand of hair, or a drop of blood. And so, I turned to the only thing that remained beside me.

"Why? Why me?" I said to the Ibli.

A sound like gurgling emitted from its throat. "I liked your bitterness, your cowardice, the taste of your pain. I wanted more."

"This is the end. The end of everything," I said, staring at the Ibli horde laying waste to Karagatan.

"Yes."

"So what will happen to me now? Will you kill me, too?"

"If you turn west."

"And east, to Karagatan?"

"Whether you die by my hand or by my brethren is of no concern to me. So long as you die."

I nodded, more out of habit than a desire to respond. But I couldn't leave it there. I had one more question that needed to be answered.

"Tell me. That world you sent me where the daylight never fails and the Iblis never were. Was it real?"

"What would make you suffer more? Being where you could never stay or craving what could never be?"

"Either way, I'm ruined."

With that, I hauled myself to my feet and stumbled off to greet my fate, to meet the Kivranmak a third time. For a moment, the Ibli watched me leave, but then it sank beneath the ground, merged into the soil. Only then did I allow myself a smile.

Toward the end of our encounter, I'd painted my face with sadness to let the Ibli think it had won. But after forty years, I'd found the reason behind the promise my parents had made to me, and Malea had made to Lawin. It was hope, a belief that even in the face of suffering better things would come, and what is dreamed and what is real would both someday be one.

So now, here at the end, this was hope to me: that I would fall asleep, and return to that world of light, where the spirit of Malea and Lawin live on. That once the Iblis find and kill my sleeping body, my tether to this world would break, and I'd remain in that better place forever. Maybe it wouldn't happen that way; my mind accepted that possibility. Nevertheless, as I headed for Karagatan, it wasn't a march toward imminent destruction. I went toward hope, borrowed from Martin, refined by love, strengthened by the memory of sunlight, and sealed by promises that I finally, finally understood.

SLEEPING CUPID WAKES

BENJIE PEERS OUTSIDE, ONE last look before the darkness comes, and with it the aberration. The shadows gathering in his back yard don't bother him, but the clouded sky—streaked in violent sunset hues—makes him almost nauseous. It reminds him of abscesses, or the pink and purple swirl of bruises, and he can't help thinking that if he peered out from some distant, mountain vantage-point, he'd find other signs of illness threading through the ground. As if the aberration were a disease, and the city an infected host oblivious to its condition.

He turns away, takes in the insides of his house, his final refuge. There's no time to get supplies, so he scavenges through rooms, tears cupboards down, rips shelves off walls, and nails the longest, strongest boards across the front and back entrance. There are too many windows to contend with. Some he covers, but the rest he shakes his head at, prays to God the flimsy plastic of the blinds will be enough. It won't be. For what's coming, nothing will suffice, but that's what prayer's all about: pleading to the sky for the impossible on the off chance something hears and answers.

After collapsing to the recliner, he turns on Danielle's favorite show. She'd recommended it to him years ago, back when they were still locked in the throes of fledgling romance. He'd never found the time to watch it, but with nothing left to do but sit and wait, what better time to start?

A fatalistic chuckle bubbles from his lips. It feels right for once, perfect for the occasion. It's the only thing he feels before his body numbs, and he sinks deep inside himself, and the only sound is the blare of Netflix streaming one last, desperate binge.

* * *

Danielle was Benjie's first girlfriend, but their relationship didn't have the legs to make it past ninth grade. High school felt too new, too exciting for her to limit herself to only one guy. Maybe they'd found true love, and maybe they'd be together again someday. But "for now" she wanted a break, needed to dip her toe into the waters of a bigger, brighter pond. Stir up all the silt and see what fish swam by.

Or, at least, that was the gist of it. Her real words were far less ostentatious: "We had something special. I can't deny that. But I'm too young to be in a serious relationship right now. I'll always treasure the time we had together, and I hope we can still be friends."

As if the Dear John letter she'd folded into thirds and stuffed into Benjie's locker wasn't bad enough, she already had a new boyfriend. Some outgoing junior who'd found his niche on the low rung of the cool ladder with class-clown antics and a penchant for double-breasted coats. He never failed to come sniffing around whenever Danielle was alone, so it was of little surprise when she admitted they were together. Not in words, but Benjie's question pitched with a shrug, and answered by a somber nod while she sat with her new beau in the quad, head pressed against his chest.

Benjie thought about suicide for weeks, pushed up against a free fall from bridges or tall buildings, or the tumult of cars careening down a busy street. Fourteen, and already finished with it all. Fourteen, and ready for what came next. He wrote her a letter explaining how much she'd hurt him, but never sent it. Instead, he lit the page on fire and tossed it in his bathroom sink and let it burn, watched it curl and blacken. Then he kept on living. Because suicide was too messy, death too scary, and besides, living was the only thing he knew.

* * *

After the breakup, Benjie didn't speak to Danielle for years. When he finally did, it wasn't some romantic reunion, the night drenched in city lights, with a triumphant symphony pouring from some storefront's speakers while they quietly embraced. They met at a corner table at Mindy's, the voice of Justin Bieber mewling from the retro jukebox parked up front.

Benjie arrived first. He sipped water from a straw, taking hungry sniffs at the smells wafting from the kitchen, while his brain simmered in nostalgia. For four years he and Danielle had walked hand-in-hand to this same restaurant after school let out. Neither of their parents thought much of their relationship. They called it "puppy love," said it was just a phase all kids went through. The crack and dazzle of fireworks before the bitty sparkles faded out. Without parental support, they couldn't have proper dates, and without driver's licenses the gap between their homes—on opposite sides of town—might as well have been a boundless gulf. That thirty-minute span before their parents picked them up was the only time they could be alone.

Reverie took a back seat the moment Danielle arrived and dropped into the chair across from him. Just like old times, she held his hand. No warning, didn't ask permission, just formed a yin-yang with their palms and squeezed. It shocked him, but no more than the brusque response his body gave: a cold shiver, racing heartbeat, and a nervousness that soaked his underarms with sweat. But regardless of what his body thought, he hadn't come because of unrequited love; that brain passenger had long since sailed off on the USS Betrayal. No, he wanted answers, plain and simple. Answers she had promised. Answers that were a long time coming.

He ordered his usual, pastrami on rye, and she still saw no problem with adding bacon to her slice of vegetarian pizza. Their conversation bordered on perfunctory—college, jobs, cars, living situations—with awkward lulls they filled with half-formed smiles and hearty gulps of Coke. Thankfully, Danielle broke the small-talk cycle first.

"All my high school boyfriends were assholes and no one better ever came along after that. It's you, Benjie. It's always been you, and I wish it hadn't taken me so long to realize it."

At least, he wished she'd said that, in some forgotten part of him, beneath scar tissue that had formed around a Danielle-shaped hole.

What she really said was, "You look different."

"Do I?"

"Yeah. Older, sure, but something else. Something I can't quite put my finger on."

"In a good way?"

"I'm not sure."

He scoffed, tried to pull his hand free, but she held on even tighter.

"Sorry. Didn't mean to offend you. I just don't know what else to say, I guess."

"I'm not offended," he lied. "But if you want a good place to begin, how about you start with why?"

"Why what?"

"Why you texted me. Why now. Why it even matters anymore."

The frown lines across her face deepened, accenting shadows beneath her eyes he hadn't realized wasn't makeup. It aged her, transformed her into a woman with the barest semblance of the girl he used to know. Whatever passive irritation he felt drained away. Because however blunt her observation, she was absolutely right: he had changed. They both had.

"Do you remember that conversation we had at school?" she asked. "It was lunchtime. We were sitting on our own, in the field beyond the bleachers. I asked you if you believed in ghosts, and you said—"

"'Kind of. Maybe. I don't know.'"

"That's right." She smiled, this time for real, red warmth coloring her cheeks. "I knew you didn't, but you never could tell me no."

He laughed. "I had this strange idea that if we ever disagreed on something, it meant we weren't a perfect match. I didn't want think about that, at least not while things were still good."

"It's not so strange. I had something I wanted to tell you that day, but I didn't because I felt embarrassed. Thought you might laugh at me, or worse, think I was crazy."

"Well? Tell me now."

Danielle's expression intensified. She took a breath and held it, and like his hand, he thought she might never let it go.

"I used to see a ghost. The first time, it was standing outside my bedroom window."

"How do you know it was a ghost?"

"Dunno. Maybe it wasn't. All I knew for sure was that it felt wrong, unnatural, an aberration. In any case, I waved. I thought if it didn't react, that would prove it wasn't really there, that it had to be a weird reflection, or some product of my mind. But soon as I did, it came closer to the window, pressed right up against the glass, and spoke."

"What did it say?"

"It said 'Cupid.' Three times."

"Okay... What did it look like?"

"I don't know, can't remember anything but rubbing my eyes, really digging into them, as if I were convinced the pain and pressure would drive the sight of it away. I screamed. My parents came to check on me, but, of course, it had vanished by then. Didn't tell them what happened, just blamed it on a nightmare. I wanted you to be the first to know, but like I said, I lost my nerve."

Benjie propped his chin up on his free hand and searched her face, trying hard to spot the cracks in her demeanor. Some small sign of a joke, a lie, or the madness she'd acknowledged might be there, but hadn't copped to yet.

"That's quite the story," he said.

"Tell me you believe it."

"No offense, but that's a big ask, all things considered."

She threw herself against her backrest, the force of it almost tipping her chair over.

"Look, Benjie, I know what I did. I'm not saying it was right, but I am saying I thought it was necessary at the time. I'm not saying I'll ever deserve your trust again, but I am saying..." The start of tears turned her eyes to glass, and her mouth snapped shut. "Never mind."

Benjie almost circled the table, almost threw his arms around her. But the need to comfort her soon faded, extinguished by a different sort of specter than the one from her delusions: a phantom of the boy who had replaced him, arms wrapped around her, forcing her head back against his chest. He bit his cheek, dabbed the pain around his eyes and mouth to simulate concern, and patted at her hand until her cry-spell ended.

"This was a mistake," she said, and stood. "I just...wanted you to understand the reasons for what happened, for why I did what I did. But I don't have the right to anymore."

She didn't give him time to respond, didn't say another word, simply collected her things and marched toward the exit with the soullessness of a mother leaving her child's funeral. One backward glance, a timid wave, and she was gone.

* * *

He fixes himself a cup of coffee, the instant kind that films his mouth with bitterness and sour. Taste doesn't matter anymore, only the boost that makes his heart beat quicker, and keeps his mind from shutting down. Not a beverage, he reminds himself, but liquid speculum for his eyes.

The night inches forward, a slow progression toward a destination it can't find and doesn't care to reach. The rain picks up, and winds crash and bully through the city streets. The house sways. Walls and floorboards creek and whimper, and hidden in the din of battered wood a sound like garbled voices seeded with his and Danielle's names.

He tells himself it isn't real, but he doesn't believe a word of it. People often fool themselves into believing the mundane is supernatural, but he can't find the mental trickery to work that same lie in reverse. He trails back into the living room, arms trembling, the freshly brewed concoction spilling on his hand. Then he sits, resumes the show.

* * *

In Benjie's dream, he and Danielle stood together on a shoreline, overlooking a sea of black water, and a red sun that melted like wax over the horizon. The razor edges of rocks cut into their feet. Monstrous things living in the ground below opened their mouths, tongues snaking up through crevices, to lap the trickles of their blood.

In reality, they'd only ever kissed. But there, in that place of unrealized possibilities, they did much more than that. She lay flat against the ground, her back and his legs carved into oblivion. While her breath caressed his neck, he quietly enfolded her, joined with her, and within the spreading shadows of a dying sun, their flesh became one.

Beads of sweat covered Benjie's forehead when he woke. A backhand to wipe it dry, and then he stood, pacing the dull confines of his bedroom in a steady line. When they were still together, he took that dream as a promise, all the violent imagery converted into symbols of their undying love. Later, it became a manifestation of his pain and regret. But now, just days after he'd met with her again, it felt dark and sinister. A looming threat.

The light of his cellphone flicked on, but he didn't notice until the delayed vibrations drilled into his bedside table. He sauntered over, picked it up. Danielle's name hovered above the words, *I'm sorry.* Seconds later, a new text appeared below it: *Despite everything that's happened, I never stopped loving you.*

He stared at it, expected any second to see, *Whoops. Color me embarrassed. Wrong number!* It had to be a mistake. He almost hit reply, to ask her to confirm it, but he stopped himself with a single thought that swept every trace of curiosity aside: too little, too late. Any day within the first year, he might have relented, might have forgiven, might have even taken her back. But eight years was too long, enough to let the good times spoil, and the bad ones seem all the more perverse. While he didn't hate her—couldn't hate her if he tried to—he was beyond forgiving, and a far way off from love.

He placed his cellphone back upon the bedside table. The green light of the alarm clock revealed it was only 6 AM. While still too early to begin his day, he'd spend the extra time in the shower, washing, scrubbing, rinsing all thought of Danielle down the drain.

* * *

Benjie never believed in ghosts, but Danielle haunted him all the same. It didn't matter what he did. He could be sleeping, driving, working, or shopping, and a part of her would creep into his mind and hold tight, like a pebble jammed into the gearwork of his brain. He wondered if that's what ghosts truly were. Not souls trapped between this world and the next, but unwanted memories that wouldn't fade and refused to be forgotten. He even began having his own ghostly experiences. Sympathetic hallucinations, he called them. Some unlikely fusion of empathy, Danielle's story, and his near obsession with their past.

The first one occurred at Benjie's work on a Friday. By evening, the office was deserted, but he'd volunteered to stay behind to finish up a project due when Monday rolled around. Mostly mindless data entry, but with the added complication of navigating the ancient computer system the company provided: duotone graphics, a text-based OS, and fat keyboard buttons with thick springs that defied all but the most persistent touch.

At half past eight, he heard footsteps trail across the vinyl carpet runner. Then he saw the reflection of something looming over his shoulder in the black sidebars of his computer screen. No details, just a crude distortion in the rough shape of a head.

He looked up, scanned around. His office space was isolated in the backroom of a single-story building. To his right, a high partition obscured the insides of his boss's corner cubicle. Spanning windows lined the front, overlooking the façade of an adjacent building, and behind him, a narrow walkway flanked the stark white, blank back wall. There was nothing he couldn't see with a single, sweeping glance, but he saw exactly that: nothing.

He heard footsteps again, this time somewhere in his boss's cubicle. A thump on the partition made it flex and wobble. He jumped to his feet—heart racing, palms sweating—and hurried to investigate the source. No one could have scrambled past him in the time it took to round the partition, but the cubicle was empty. The only signs of an intrusion were papers strewn across the floor, and the computer chair's seat caught halfway in a swivel.

The second one occurred when he visited a friend's house that Saturday evening. Soon as moonlight dallied beyond the curtains, Benjie caught a figure trudging up the staircase from the corner of his eye—gone before he could even blink. Later, his keys translocated from the coffee table to the kitchen counter, and the shoes he'd left on the tile of the entryway flew across the room. Toward the end of his visit, something heavy clomped through an empty room upstairs—though his friend swore up and down he had no visitors, and his roommates had left the townhouse earlier that day.

By the third occurrence, Benjie allowed himself to believe something more was at play than a rampaging imagination, that Danielle's supernatural visitor might actually be real. A late-night video game session after work dragged him into the early morning hours. When he finally called it quits, he stumbled down the hall into his bedroom, and crawled half-conscious into bed. He barely noticed the slow eclipse of moonlight streaming through his open curtains. Thought it was a passing car, if he even put his mind to it. The room went cold. His breath dawdled in clouds before his face, but it took a squeak—the sound of wet fingers rubbing glass—before he bothered looking up.

Something watched Benjie through his bedroom window, its body cloaked in shadow, barely more than a silhouette. Upturned shoulders or a hunch swallowed any sign of neck, its smooth head perched upon its frame like a melon in a shallow serving bowl. If it had a face, Benjie couldn't see it. But it must have had a mouth, because when it spoke, he could hear the wet crinkle of a tongue slide against its palate.

"Cu-pid, how long are your claws. Cu-pid, how strong are your jaws. Cut out my lover's heart for meeeeeeee."

Its breathless, high-pitched voice had a gummed-up pronunciation that hinted at a smile. The words could have been a song, save for the absence of a melody. In fact, a memory stirred of some golden oldie his parents might have listened to, now long since relegated to the trash bin of his mind.

The figure pushed a finger at the windowpane. The glass squealed as the nail carved an M, then a V below it, lengthening the outer lines so that they met. It was a rudimentary heart. Thick strokes with jagged edges, drawn with dumb simplicity or a madman's disregard. It watched Benjie for a moment, head cocked, its finger now tapping at the glass like a child prodding a reaction from a caged animal.

Benjie couldn't speak, had regressed into a shocked state beyond all thought or capacity for fight or flight. Drool trickled from his slackened jaw. His breath hitched in his chest, but nothing, not the insanity unfolding or the burning of his lungs, could stir him into action.

The figure chuckled and backed away. A chiseled smile of glowing, yellow teeth appeared, and the blotted thing sidled out of sight. Moonlight streamed into Benjie's bedroom once again, just as the central heat kicked on with a clunk and whirr. It took an hour of numb and mindless writhing before warmth returned to his extremities, and with it a calm that restored him to his senses.

Somehow, he managed to fall asleep. But all his dreams were fevered and monotonous, a cavalcade of disconnected scenes in which he ran through a vast expanse of darkness, while the figure—that thing, that aberration—chased him.

* * *

He didn't go to work later that day, didn't even bother calling in. The shock of the early morning had drained him in ways he didn't understand. He didn't feel tired so much as weak and disoriented, and spent the brunt of the afternoon stumbling through his house, the rooms spinning, the walls swirling and stretching like the contents of a funhouse mirror.

Despite it all, he took comfort in the visitation. In some strange way, it made him feel closer to Danielle, as if they were special: two explorers converging on a lonely road, facing down a mystery in the distance that defied all bounds of reason. The implications thrilled him. He pictured himself at Mindy's holding Danielle's hand as they spent hours trying to disambiguate what the aberration was, and what it meant for them.

Soon as he showered, dressed, and ate a modest meal, he texted her: *Hey, Danielle, sorry for not responding sooner, but you gave me a lot to digest. I was also thinking about the story you told me. How about we meet up again today and talk. Same bat time, same bat channel?*

The response came at once: *Benjie?*

Yeah.

Benjie Mapili from Danielle's high school?

He shook his head, a fit of irritation mounting inside him. Was this some kind of game, or a brazen case of gaslighting? Either way, he didn't like it.

Uh, yeah. Still me. Look, this is serious. Weird things keep happening, and you're the only one I know that seems to know what's going on.

Minutes passed, and then: *This isn't Danielle, it's her father. I'm sorry, but Danielle passed away last night.*

* * *

No one contacted Benjie about Danielle's funeral, but he took the announcement of her wake—printed in the local newspaper—as an open invitation. The ceremony was to be held at her parents' house. Address undisclosed, but he knew where to find it, had passed it numerous times as a child while driving as a passenger in his parents' car. The heart pounding realization that his first crush, and then first girlfriend lived there, followed by the soul-wrenching, slow-sinking truth that his first ex lived there too. He couldn't help but memorize its location. It was an X carved into the mental map of his hometown, which, like Danielle, could never be erased.

Benjie wore his best suit, and cleaned and polished up his only pair of loafers. When they dated, he and Danielle never had an opportunity to get dressed up. She got sick the day of their eighth-grade dance, and his parents had taken him on vacation during the week of their freshman winter ball.

It seemed an odd thing to regret missing out on childhood dances so many years beyond the fact, but he did. Because she had. Because she'd cried both times they'd missed their chance, and his promise of an unforgettable junior and senior prom had never come to fruition. He only hoped this would make up for it. That if she could have seen him in his three-piece suit, and her in her gray, floral sequined gown, she would have loved it, would have even smiled.

Those in attendance faced away from Danielle's coffin, a two-ton elephant they didn't dare acknowledge. They stood in groups of mostly twos and threes, keeping conversations calm and quiet, and suitable for mourning. The majority of their children roistered in the back yard, playing with whatever amenities a house meant only for adults provided. Benjie paced the perimeter of the living room, avoiding stares that probed his passing, trying to evince the air of someone who belonged.

Once in a while, he snuck glances at Danielle's neglected body. Her coffin, hoisted by a catafalque, had been set against the living room's back wall, surrounded by rug impressions left by an enormous entertainment center long since lugged into some unseen back room. She looked beautiful, serene, but also wrong in ways he couldn't wrap his mind around. As if the part of her that left had taken pieces of him with it, and the emptiness he saw reflected a deeper truth about himself.

He wanted to go to her, even had sad, desperate daydreams where she wasn't gone, but merely sleeping. Snow White lying in a poisoned slumber, waiting for her prince to wake her with a kiss. But the greater part of him wanted to leave, to pass the burden of remorse onto someone else's shoulders. Anyone would do. Some crush, an infrequent lover, maybe even a close friend—but not the ex-boyfriend eight years removed. He'd earned his peace through the suffering of her rejection, had cried enough to cover even this, her death.

"But it has to be you, Benjie. Because you loved her. Because you love her even now, more than anyone ever did."

Benjie spun around, darted glances in every direction. The idea had tickled the underside of his brain for a week now, but he never dreamed of owning it, didn't have the courage to admit it, much less speak the words aloud. And yet, it had been spoken. The pronouncement whispered in his ear by someone in this very house.

He searched the faces of all the people present, trying to discern the difference between expressions that might have been guilt or gloom. That was when he saw it: the aberration leaning beside the doorway to the kitchen, body flickering, as if its existence battled with annihilation for the upper hand. Even at the peak of clarity, he could tell nothing of its features. It could have been anyone or anything with humanoid proportions, as if the fine details were being filtered through a pane of frosted glass.

"Cu-pid, how long are your claws," the aberration said, its strained syllables dripping with an overeager tone. "Cu-pid, how strong are your jaws." Something that must have been a mouth widened and then snapped shut. It dragged a hand across the left side of its chest, and then, "Cut out my lover's heart for meeeeeeee."

While Danielle's obituary had implied a natural death, Benjie had suspected the aberration from the start. Its gloating recitation only confirmed it. He lunged, not caring for the distance between them, knowing only the bestial need to wrap his fingers around its throat. The aberration vanished soon as he took a step. Seconds later, it appeared around a corner of the hallway on the opposite side of the room, finger wagging with admonishment.

"Cu-pid. Cu-pid. Cu-pid," it taunted, and then ducked through the nearest open door as soon as Benjie charged again.

Benjie scanned the room, angling to peer around the motion of the crowd. When he found it next, it stood beside the coffin, hunched over Danielle's body. Elbows raised, it swayed from side to side, arms lashing out with mechanical precision, devoted to a single task. Morbid curiosity filled him, even as his insides churned with hate, revulsion. When it finally stood erect again, it turned. One last glance at Benjie before the crowd folded in, obstructing the sight of another ghastly, yellow smile.

"Benjie?"

Benjie jolted, pivoted while covering his face, expecting the aberration to attack him the same way it had just attacked Danielle. But only Danielle's mother stood beside him. Embarrassment won out over the shiver of relief he felt, and his cheeks burned as he struggled to compose himself.

"I didn't think I'd see you here," she said.

"I'm sorry. I know I wasn't invited, but—"

She shook her head. "If the thought had occurred to John or me, you can be sure we would have invited you. Danielle never stopped talking about you, even near the end. 'The one that got away,' as it were."

"I don't understand."

"She was devastated when you broke up with her, but she kept you in her heart all the same. What I'm saying is you deserve to be here as much as anybody else."

"But... she broke up with me."

"Did she?" She shrugged, her expression one of cold detachment. "You'd know better than me, of course, but that's not how she described it. A misunderstanding, perhaps? Alas. The ways of a young heart." She reached out, and the ghost of fingers barely grazed his shoulder. "Thanks again for coming," she said, and continued on her way.

Benjie turned back to the coffin. The crowd had finally parted, allowing a clear view of Danielle's body. The aberration had carved her hair and face away, leaving only glistening muscle, cartilage, and the round orbs of her eyes staring out in counterfeit awareness. What's more, a gaping hole had been punched into her chest. While he couldn't see the extent of the damage, based on its placement and the aberration's words, he could guess at what it meant: it'd taken her heart as well.

He choked back the need to vomit, had only sense enough to back away, slowly, slowly, so as not to draw any attention. Or the blame. Once her family noticed what had happened, there'd be hell to pay, and the uninvited stranger in their midst would make the perfect target. But when he found the entryway, panic mode set in and he bullied through the front door, racing with wild abandon in the direction of his car.

* * *

He grips the hammer hidden inside the flap of his jacket, cold steel muted by a rubber handle. Something sharp slides against the outside kitchen wall, a disconcerting sound like nails on a chalkboard, or flatware scraping Styrofoam. His chest stutters, and his eyes roll back, and he tries to plug his ears to keep out what's coming next, but it's too late. It's in there, rattling the contents of his head, sewing fear in the soil of his mind.

"Cu-pid, how long are your claws. Cu-pid, how strong are your jaws. Cut out my lover's heart for meeeeeeee."

He sinks, curls into his chair and cries. For a man who hasn't cried in years, it's a mild relief mixed with near debilitating shame. He always thought he'd be strong in the end, thought he'd be the type to stare straight into the shadow beneath the Grim Reaper's hood. Give that demon a cocksure smile before it snatched his soul away. But he's not sure of anything right now, not even if he can pass the night without soiling his slacks, back to front.

Why did she have to start loving him again, he wonders with the ferocity of an accusation.

The question eats at him, a swarm of starved rats gnawing through his stomach. He wants to vomit, wants to fall asleep, but his body won't comply with either. Because the noise coming from the outside kitchen wall is growing louder, more violent, until it's no longer just the aberration's voice and scratching, but boards and wires and insulation being ripped out from his house.

"Cu-pid. Cu-pid. Cu-pid," he hears the aberration chant. Over and over, the needle of a record stuck on a one-word groove.

Why did he have to love her back, he also wonders, the thought calmer, but no less unkind.

If love were an eye, he would gladly pluck it from its socket. If he could extract his feelings for her like a parasite, he'd do so, and crush it between his fingers. He could feign disgust, spit every hateful word conjured forth by his imagination, but it wouldn't help, wouldn't change a thing. His heart would know the truth about the way he felt for Danielle—and so would the aberration.

* * *

Before the long drive back to his house, he stopped by Mindy's. It seemed like the right thing to do. The events set in motion by his and Danielle's meeting were coming to a close, and Mindy's had played a part in it: the place where it began, the place where it resumed, and now the place where it would likely end.

Soon as he stepped inside, the rattle of a full kitchen competed with the raucous chatter of an early dinner crowd. A grandmother feeding a fistful of quarters to the jukebox only made it worse, and soon McCartney's familiar tenor belted "Hey Jude" from the wall-mounted speakers. Patrons crammed every seat and table, but it didn't matter to Benjie. He didn't intend to stay for longer than he had to.

The girl behind the register greeted him with a grin, a tip-me smile that showed too many of her yellow smoker's teeth. It reminded him of the aberration.

"Give me a large pizza to go," he said, averting his eyes to the register's display. "Vegetarian with bacon."

"It'll be about thirty minutes."

"Fine. Whatever." He slapped a twenty on the counter. "But quicker if you can. I'm in a hurry."

She scoffed, and her eyes widened like her smile. He couldn't stop himself from thinking of Danielle's bulging stare, so he turned to face the dining room. A family vacated a table just feet from where he stood. With nothing else to do, he slipped into the closest chair, then plucked the cellphone from his pocket to scroll through Danielle's texts. The first one he had all but memorized by now.

If you ever still wonder why we broke up, I'm finally ready to talk.

He never saw that coming. It was the last thing he ever expected to read from the last person he ever expected to hear from. Twice so when she'd written, *Despite everything that's happened, I never stopped loving you.*

He wanted to believe her; it had a cruel, sad sense of poetry about it. If not the quality of a Shakespearean romantic tragedy, then at least a passing homage. Nevertheless, her heartfelt declaration seemed inconsistent with the facts. She had to have stopped loving him. Only the rekindling of his feelings had placed him in the center of the aberration's crosshairs, and her death had followed too soon after her last profession to be a matter of pure chance.

With the scant evidence at his disposal, a narrative formed of a beast—an anti-Cupid—following the trail of true love, stalking its practitioners, until death was the inevitable result. Maybe *it* had caused their breakup. Maybe the fear of *it* had made her wait. And maybe, after all these years, she began to feel safe again, took a chance to heal old wounds, and it all spiraled down from there.

The music stopped. A brief flutter from the jukebox and a new record drifted into place. Benjie knew the tune at once, but he couldn't quite place it until the singing started. "Cupid," a Sam Cooke classic. Different lyrics, but the same basic rhythm as the aberration's twisted recitation. When the song rounded on its second verse, it stalled, Sam Cooke crooning, "Cupid, Cupid, Cupid," almost like a chant.

The girl who'd taken Benjie's order announced a number, followed by his name. He stared at her, too dazed to comprehend the meaning. When he finally did, he stumbled to the counter on the warm taffy of his legs, grabbed the pizza, scrambled for the exit, and left that place—with all its squashed hopes and ruined memories—behind.

Within minutes after leaving, Benjie saw glimpses of Danielle everywhere: standing in the center of a crowd, walking past the window of a grocery store, climbing through the rubble of a vacant lot. He even saw her seated in the backseat through the rearview mirror, hair covering her eyes, the soft, white skin of her cheeks. One quick glance, and she was gone. Only the after-image, burned into his mind, revealed the truth. She wasn't whole, just a mask worn above the blurred and flickering semblance of a body.

When he arrived home, he slammed the door, and locked and bolted it. He hurried to the family room, stopped to toss the pizza on the coffee table, and locked and bolted the back door as well. Then he peered through the blinds of the closest window, searching for a sign. One last look before the darkness came, and with it the aberration.

* * *

Benjie listens to the tapping at his bedroom door, a sound boisterous as a thunderclap in the hanging silence of the living room. Adrenaline kicks in, a swirling force of cold and nervous energy that makes his skin tingle and sweat drip down his face. His mind races, begging him to take his car and flee, with the vague promise of asylum and the countless miles of unobstructed roads he needs to get there. But after all that's happened, he knows running would be pointless. It'd only find him. It always does.

A door squeals open. Steady scuffing trails a soft patter, as if the aberration is crawling along the carpet of his bedroom floor. Mattress springs bounce and creak, and the aberration changes course again, surging down the hall the way it came. Benjie grips his recliner's armrests tighter, fingers sinking into leather knuckles deep, and peers back just as it rounds the corner of the living room. It rises from all fours within the doorway. It still wears a mask of

Danielle's skin, disheveled hair framing black and empty sockets, sagging lips parted like she wants to speak.

"Run," he wishes she would say. "I love you too much to let you die this way."

But she doesn't. Because she's gone. Because the true her is rotting in a coffin thirty miles away, and she'll never look at him, smile at him, or say another word again.

Benjie forces his fingers to make a fist around the hammer's handle, and then searches for his will to fight, tries to connect with that primal need for life—anything but the fear and grief that keeps him rooted to his chair. He grunts, straightens his jacket, tightens his tie. His appetite left hours ago, but he takes the final slice of pizza and nibbles quiet as a mouse along its edges.

That movement is all it takes. The aberration scuttles up behind him, arms held wide, head bobbing like a limp weight. Benjie twists around and swings, and the hammer soars. The steel claw scoops furrows from the aberration's cheek. Another blow against its temple earns a hopeful crack, and drives it to its knees. But it's not good enough by far; the aberration is too quick. In a seamless stream of motion, it rises to its feet, swats the tool aside, and embraces Benjie.

It moans, deep and throaty. Fingers caress his back, a mockery of intimacy that makes his arms flare up in goosebumps. It smiles down at him, mask stretching, conforming to the muscles shifting underneath, until its cheeks split in crooked lines that let the yellow of its grin shine through.

An invisible force locks around Benjie's wrists, steering his hand so that it pressed against the creature's sternum. He feels a heartbeat, quick but steady—not hammering with adrenaline like a predator that's caught its prey, but the gentle patter of a nervous lover. Her heart, he realizes. Dead but somehow living in this monster's chest.

Benjie tries to break free from the aberration's grip, but he can't. His shaking, aching limbs can only flail by mere inches, and he's forced to stare into the sallow ruin of Danielle's face. The end is near, but he can't smirk, only choke, and gasp, and sob, and even his last attempt to speak Danielle's name comes out in whimpers.

The aberration looms closer.

"Cu-pid, Cu-pid, Cu-pid."

One final chant. A sick, sweet whisper in Benjie's ear before its claws dig deep, and a suffocating darkness spreads.

PLASTIC LOVE

JARED SPENT THE MORNING wandering his house, listening to the heaving sobs his body made with a clinician's cold detachment. It wasn't that he couldn't understand the reasons for his grief; it was the scope that separated his mind from the raw, base emotions of his body. His mother had died. They'd scheduled her funeral for six that evening. Pain was pain, but he could more easily comprehend the form and structure of the universe than fathom the eternal absence of the one who gave him life.

He glanced at his wristwatch. After rubbing at his itching, red-rimmed eyes before his bathroom mirror, he shuffled to the back porch and collapsed onto his rocker. He glanced at his wristwatch again. Only two minutes had passed since last he checked, but it felt like so much more.

Time was never quite as nebulous as when you missed someone, their absence like a clock without any hands or numbers. Even seconds lagged, stretching well beyond their proper measure. To pass the near eternity of the moment, he watched a dragonfly flitter through his back yard. It hurtled past the raised garden beds, strafed the dried remains of Jared's long-neglected lawn, and perched on a sunflower mere inches from where he sat.

As a child, Jared often wondered how flying things could fly. His mother told him it had something to do with lift and thrust and drag, but he never believed it. Not really. He'd never found evidence to dispel the notion either, but he kept watching, hoping to see past the illusion to the truth hiding underneath.

The dragonfly's wings twitched. Jared held his breath, watched it all the harder. As the insect rose, he finally saw what he'd been waiting for all these years: a bit of sunlight reflecting off a thin, transparent thread fixed to the center of the dragonfly's back. A thread that stretched up and up and up, like a towline tethered to the heavens.

At once, the world transformed around him: pipe cleaner trees, popsicle stick fences, felt lawns, building-block houses. Some vinyl thing—a neighbor—leaned over the fence between their properties, enough to reveal its face. It smiled with painted lips framing a seamless barricade of teeth. With its stiff arm raised in greeting, its body tottered side to side, as if shaken in some unseen child's grip.

Good afternoon! Afternoon!

"Hi, Bill," said Jared.

I'm sorry to hear about your mother's passing. Passing. You must really miss her. Miss her.

Jared was never the type to talk about his feelings, especially when he couldn't quite connect with them himself. He grunted. A brief silence, and Doll Bill stared into the sky.

Sure is some heat wave we're having. Having.

Jared held his palm out, cupping the harsh, hot sunlight as if it were a spat of rain. "It's a boy's craft world baking in his parents' oven. That's all."

It wasn't funny, but Jared laughed. Doll Bill chortled even louder, the unseen child shaking its vinyl body harder than before. Soon as the laughter stalled, the world reinstated. Trees became wood, fences became oak pickets, and Doll Bill reverted back to flesh again. But the real Bill wasn't laughing, only smiling, only staring at Jared with deep blue eyes that wouldn't blink. It took a second, but Jared recognized those eyes. They were the same color as his mother's.

* * *

In third grade, Jared left his school craft project on his father's desk. The den was off limits, his father's sole domain, but he wanted it to be a surprise and show off all the hard work he'd done. "Our Neighborhood," he called it. The next time he found the thing, it was a pile of broken scraps smoldering on the stovetop.

"Do you ever wonder what it'd be like if it were only you and me?" his mother whispered while she rocked him into sleep that evening. "What if we went somewhere? Would you like that?"

"Where would we go?" asked Jared, still devastated by his loss.

His mother shrugged, eyebrows furrowed, face full of quiet contemplation. "Who cares? So long as we're together."

* * *

Jared's mother called his father Big Man.

"Three reasons," she had admitted, though she seemed to have no intention of sharing them.

When Jared was young, the mere existence of an answer he should have known—but didn't—made him anxious, and nothing could persuade him to relent. For months, he tried to guess her reasons, sometimes pacing through the living room, sometimes lying on the couch, or sprawled out on his bed. When he thought of something, he'd tear through the house until he found her, a grin heralding his purpose before he even spoke.

Was it because no matter how far he reached his arms around his father, he could never touch his fingers on the other side?

Was it because he had to step up on his tippy toes and tilt his head back to look into his father's eyes?

His father was a mountain spanning the horizon, tall enough to scratch the underbelly of the clouds, and that's what made him Big Man, right?

"That's part of it," she admitted.

"Well, what else?"

His mother winked and nodded. It took years before Jared understood that answer, and by then he wished he hadn't. The last reason he regretted most of all, and it was this: Big Man was strong, Big Man was loud, and Big Man never let his tiny, quiet wife forget it. The telltale signs were there, but whenever Jared started noticing, his father always had a reason to make it seem all right.

"Sometimes daddies get angry," his father explained, with little Jared bouncing on his knee. "Sometimes mothers run their mouths and we have to remind them of their place. Same as you. Sometimes you run your mouth and what do I do?"

"Spank me."

"That's it right there. It isn't okay for a wife or son to make a man feel small inside. You understand?"

"So you spank Mom too?"

"Something like that. It's different for adults. The ass doesn't hurt as much as other things."

That part was true: never the ass. Whenever Big Man's bouts of steam-fueled rage came on, anything was game but that. Mostly the face, or arms, or parts of her body no good and decent son would ever see—outside of swimwear. Jared wished he never accepted this, but he had. Because Big Man, first of his name, King of the Household, Lord of the Garage and Den had spoken, and he was never wrong. Not once in all his years.

* * *

Jared wrapped a silk black tie around his neck while sitting on the edge of his bed. For a moment, he considered pulling on the narrow end, cutting off the circulation to his brain. Maybe he would record it, let it stream live, the following note tucked into the description box below it:

> See the incredible choking man. Watch him swell. Watch his face redden. Watch white flecks of spit spray from his mouth, and the drool run down his chin until he's dead, dead, dead.

It would be a phenomenon, a viral hit. One million views within the first few hours. Instead, Jared tied a Windsor knot, but only pulled it tight enough to hurt, not choke. His mother didn't raise a quitter. She led by example, never giving in to thoughts of hopelessness or suicide despite seven years struggling with cancer. Or, for that matter, forty-two years struggling with Big Man.

As Jared finished lacing up his slick, black shoes, he recalled his mother's final days, and their final conversation. He'd hunched over her bedside, trying to memorize the feel and pressure of what would be their last embrace. Renal failure had turned her into the color of an overripe lemon. She didn't eat, could barely breathe by then. Neither of them bothered to pretend she had much time left.

Once the hospice nurse left the room, to give them a moment of privacy, Jared's mother took his hand and told him, "Look for me after I die. I'll be up there in the heavens. A shining star, watching and loving you forever."

Reason and evidence told him that's not how star formation worked, but he wanted to believe it. After all, if the multiverse were real, maybe that's how things worked in one of them. The fire of the soul igniting dust and gas into a semi-conscious ball of light. Regardless, it comforted him to think that she would endure, adding just a bit of illumination to when the world was at its darkest.

Big Man had a different point of view, of course. He once said that all the stars we see are dead, a billion corpses littering a graveyard of the night.

"How can that be true?" a still-young Jared asked.

"Imagine a man screaming as he's shot. Instant death, but the sound travels some distance before it finally fades away. That's stars, too. They're gone, but dead don't always know it."

Once Jared stepped outside, he was surprised to see the sun had almost set. Already a herd of stars punched through the evening's graying haze, shepherded by a waning crescent. The sodium glow of streetlamps lined both sides of the street, like torches lit in honor of the daylight's early passing.

Before he climbed into his car, he spotted the dragonfly-on-a-thread again. This time it hovered above his head, and then darted, rounding the corner of his house. The world transformed: clouds of cotton balls, gray construction paper sky, and all the houses made of plastic logs that snapped together. Another vinyl thing—this time his next-door neighbor on the other side—leaned out from its front door. Doll Tina. Like Bill, it wore his mother's deep blue eyes, a rigid arm probing at the air in something like a greeting.

Heading to your mother's funeral? Funeral?

"Yeah," said Jared. He'd never told Tina that his mother had died. He'd never told Bill either, but with everything that was happening that day, it seemed like such a minor detail to protest. "The whole family's coming. Uncles and aunts that never call or visit. Cousins I haven't seen since they were born. Should be fun."

Doll Tina watched him, its pale face accented by the stark black of its polyester hair. It leaned farther out the door and its bathrobe slipped open. A black and blue marble glaze covered its exposed body. Painted bruises accented by a red lump fixed halfway between the smooth surface of its breasts and the barest dimple of its navel. It quickly covered up.

On a lighter note, got any big plans for this weekend? Weekend?

Jared struck his car's hood with the flat of his palm, his mood balanced on the fine lines between grief and guilt, regret and anger.

"The young boy only wants to play, but all his toys were melted."

This time he didn't laugh. Neither did Doll Tina. He closed his eyes, tried to clear the thick malaise his thoughts trudged through, and when he opened them again, the vinyl thing had vanished. Tina's door was shut, her house lights off, and all the curtains drawn up tight. He grimaced, didn't wait around long enough to find out what would happen next.

* * *

At ten, Jared found his favorite toys gathered in a heap on the front lawn. Their clothes were singed, with nothing of their faces left but blackened clumps and craters. "Little boys shouldn't play with dolls," his father had explained, still wielding the magnifying glass he'd used to melt them.

To console Jared, his mother took him to the kitchen. She made him a big glass of chocolate milk, and held him as he drank it.

"If I had the power, I'd take your pain away," she said. "Or at least take you somewhere safe, where no one could ever hurt you again."

Jared merely cried, and stared, and nodded.

* * *

The drive to the cemetery was a tug-of-war between absurdity and reality, and neither had the upper hand. Dots of glitter glue sparkled from on high. The freeway changed from black velvet to asphalt, depending on the stretch of road he took. Cars whipped past him on the left, including a procession of military trucks where half the occupants were real and the other half toy soldiers.

When he arrived at the cemetery, the absurdity receded along with the last remaining sunlight. Cars packed the parking spaces closest to the cemetery's entrance, their insides brimming with shadows. In the distance, portable floodlights lined the perimeter of his mother's funeral site. His family filled rows of folding metal chairs, facing a broad canopy, with his father seated in his favorite padded lawn chair "throne" up front.

The sight of them startled Jared, if only for what they meant. This was it: the last time he would ever see his mother. The woman who had kissed his bruises to take the pain away. The woman who had fed him, bathed him, dressed him, and never once complained. His father had tried dragging him down the road to becoming Big Man 2.0, but his mother's love had saved him, set him on a higher path to...if not quite righteousness, then at least something far kinder.

He ambled through the entrance gate, taking careful steps, a stream of tears already beginning. Once he arrived at the funeral site, he made straight for the front, ignoring hands that reached for him, and somber voices offering condolences. Despite his sadness, he couldn't help but frown at the spectacle he saw: a metallic silver coffin with gold-plated hardware; oodles of floral arrangements on wire frames, accented by strings of light; a 36" by 48" canvas photo of his mother, its frame leaned up on a wooden easel. Not to mention a microphone and speakers, a stereo for music, and a generator to make them work.

His mother hadn't said much about her funeral expectations, but she had said this: "Wrap me in a newspaper and toss me in a hole. Don't make a big to-do about it. Money's for the living, so keep it. Use it for something that makes you happy." She was always practical about such things. Meaning mattered; substance over show. There was nothing about this funeral she wouldn't have hated.

Jared rounded on his father, the sun-dried grass crackling beneath his stomping feet. "You had one last chance to do right by her and you even screwed that up."

His father smoothed the collar of his favorite houndstooth jacket. He avoided Jared's gaze, offered a pained, embarrassed smile of apology to those who were seated closest.

"What's the matter, 'Big Man'?" asked Jared. "Finally at a loss for words?"

"Son," his father said, the snarl hiding in his voice wanting to be more than just a whisper. "I don't know what you're implying, but this is neither the time nor place."

"I'm not implying anything. For once in my life, I'm stating things loud and clear." Jared took three more steps, and jabbed a finger at his father's face. "This was supposed to be a modest, intimate funeral, and you made it into a goddamn three-ring circus."

Jared's father jumped to his feet. Sweat collected on his forehead, the subtle trembling of his jaw belying his hands' placating gesture. Even in his old age he was much taller than Jared, with weight to throw around—which he used right then, pushing Jared back with a thrust from his solid, bulging belly.

"That wasn't hers to ask. A funeral isn't for the dead, it's for the living. She was my wife. If this is how I choose to say goodbye, that's nobody's concern but mine."

Jared scoffed, folded his arms. "Even in the end, it all comes down to you. What Big Man wants, Big Man always gets."

"I *loved—*"

"Don't you dare say that word!" Jared shouted. "You didn't love her. She was property to you: something to shape or fix to whatever you desired. If you had truly loved her, you wouldn't have done what you did."

"So now you're going to lecture me about relationships? A single man of forty is going to tell me what true love really is?" He glanced around, raised his hands to address the family, most of them murmuring, shifting nervously in their seats. "Better listen up, folks. Pastor Jared's going to honor us with an impromptu sermon."

"No. I failed her too; we *all* did. Any one of us could have done something, could have tried and intervened. But the not-so-secret family secret had to be maintained." He threw a withering glance into the crowd, then looked over at his mother, taking in the waxy sheen of her skin, cheeks that never looked so pink in life. "What we had for Mom was plastic love. The shape and size of the real thing, but it was always fake."

A flicking like shuffled cards and the dragonfly returned, this time listing on its thread. It made a beeline for Jared, but he ducked, and it swerved and settled on the canopy. It wasn't real any longer, but a plastic toy, the kind one might find stuffed into a cardboard bin at a dollar store. The line attached to its back no longer stretched into the sky; it draped over the assembly, coiling around their legs and feet before snaking up and disappearing inside the coffin.

Jared's family had changed as well; every last one of them was a vinyl thing. They muttered words of consolation. All the empty phrases from when Jared had arrived, but so much more fitting now that they were sliding though the lips of vinyl faces.

God must have needed another angel. Angel.

Death is but a doorway to another life. Life.

Everything happens for a reason. Reason.

Even Jared's father had changed, though Doll Big Man was different from the rest in that it had kept its same proportions. It jerked sideways, feet dragging on the ground, and centered itself before the rows of its doll family.

Let us pray. Us pray.

Everyone but Jared did as commanded: heads bowed limply on

their ball joint necks, but their eyes still wide, their lips still smiling. As Doll Big Man spoke, a beam of light—like a column, big enough to bear the sky—enveloped it. The light tapered to a sliver point that inched up to Doll Big Man's cheek. Its face began to darken, to smoke, to droop. Flesh-tone vinyl dribbled down its neck, and a gaping crater formed, uncovering the hollow inside its head.

The light transferred to Doll Aunt Margaret in the back row next, and its face smoked and blistered all the same. It groaned and howled, even as the light shifted to Cousin Joseph. Then to Uncle Mike, then Grandpa Louis, then Cousin Jana, and on, and on, and on, destroying each new face one right after the other.

Jared watched everything unfold in quiet consternation. He took the briefest moment to touch his own cheek, press his stomach, and squeeze a thigh. For some reason, he was still soft, flexible, human. That was all the information he needed before he fled in the direction of his car.

He barely circled the outer edge of the funeral site when a strange glow fell upon him. He looked up. The stars had changed into a host of deep blue eyes, all dancing in a construction paper sky set on fire. The eyes loomed heavy, as if sagging from their burning perches. The pressure of their collective stare was like a surge in gravity. It made Jared falter, almost drove him to his knees, but an invisible force—the unseen child's hand—locked around his arms and waist, and held him. No matter how hard he struggled, he couldn't move, save for the useless flailing of his legs, and the pain of swollen fear coursing through his narrow veins.

The sound of something course dragging over cloth skittered from the canopy behind him. The unseen child twisted him around. His mother now sat upright in her coffin, slumped to one side, as if she had woken from a sleep, but wasn't fully conscious. Somehow she'd returned. Somehow she was alive. The shock that flooded Jared calmed his frenzied panic, and all he could think was that he had to go to her.

"Get off me," he said, thrashing in the grip that trapped him. "Let me—"

His body rose, hovered inches above the ground. Slowly, he drifted toward his mother's coffin.

"Mom? It's me, Jared."

At the sound of his voice, his mother's eyelids fluttered.

"Mom, I'm here!"

Her eyelids snapped open. Behind the spurs of her transparent eye caps, darkness stirred inside of empty sockets. She beckoned with a finger. A thin, crooked smile spread across her face, but then her lower jaw fell wide, revealing the frayed ends of threads meant to cinch her mouth shut.

My Son! My Son!

Jared screamed. The groans and shrieks of his melting family crescendoed, merging with his pleas for help, enveloping his body until it was all he heard, all he felt, the only thing he knew. As he drifted ever closer to the coffin, his mother's eager gaze devoured him. She reached out, body shaking, fingers curling, every muscle straining as if for one more last embrace.

* * *

They had a dog named Molly, a long-haired Shih Tzu that wore a pink bowtie in the center of its head. Big Man always screamed at Molly for defecating on the lawn. Then, one day, he drove her to the local vet on the pretense of vaccinations. She never came home again.

Jared's mother got another bruise for threatening to leave that night. She called to Jared when Big Man left the house to "cool down and calm his nerves." But Jared hid, refused to go to her, wouldn't do more than listen to her cry. All the while, he wondered why she always had to start things, why she always had to make his father feel so mad.

* * *

Jared slumped halfway into the coffin, his feet the only anchor to solid ground. His mother's arms enfolded him, but it was nothing like a vengeful corpse ravaging its victim. There was tenderness to her touch, a pressure that Jared recognized as uniquely hers. He didn't have the heart to struggle, so he let go, gave up, yielded to her embrace.

"I'm sorry, Mom," he said, voice so soft he could barely feel it passing from his throat.

Time passed in spurts and stutters, its measure lost within the tumult of his guilt and sadness. But he knew the world had changed back again when his mother went slack within his arms, and the strength and warmth bled out of her. A gasp escaped him when he turned and saw the devastation of his family. Only half of the attendants had survived. They kneeled beside the bodies of the newly dead, eyes averted from the charcoal holes that had once been their loved ones' faces.

Whether from shock, or grief, or some invisible force only they could feel, no one moved when Jared stooped to heave his mother's body. And when he carried her like a baby in his arms across the cemetery grounds, none of them protested, or even made a sound. He had no idea where he was going, but he knew he had to take his mother far away. He'd find a better place to bury her. Some isolated woods beyond the city limits, where litterfall would hide the loose dirt of her grave, and only a single stone would mark her place. She'd like that. A modest funeral was the only thing she'd wanted—apart from the years of aching need to get away.

"I'm so sorry," he said. "But it'll get better from here on out. It'll be exactly like you wanted: just you and me together."

As he shuffled farther from the glare of the funeral's light, he tried not to notice the smile tucked into the corner of his mother's lips, or the length of thread clasped inside her hand. Something small and plastic scuffled through the grass behind him, but he ignored that too. For once, he didn't need to know the answer. He kept his focus solely on his progress, dodging the deep black shadows of trees and tombstones, threading farther into the darkness of a starless, moonless night.

WINTER FEVER

NICHOLAS SCOOPED ANOTHER SHOVELFUL of snow from off his front yard walkway. The quiet and emptiness of his property—miles of grass and sedge buried by the previous day's flurry—made it a solemn act. Like a gravedigger, he felt obliged to shut his mouth and keep his head down until the task was finished.

He wiped sweat from his forehead, all too aware of the coming night. Ever since he was a child, he'd been afraid of the dark. No, for a man pushing forty, "afraid" was too neat, too birthday present tied in ribbon and topped with a giant, red bow. One might be "afraid" when they couldn't make it to a social function, or "afraid" they left the stove on. But darkness terrified him to his core, triggered a primordial dread deep inside him that shut off all capacity for reason and logic.

Even now—as the fading sunlight caused the shadows of his house to warp and stretch—he couldn't stop himself from thinking the outline of the chimney was a black hand grasping for his ankles, and no amount of backward glances would make the feeling go away. He paused, turned toward his house and the comfort of its familiar shape. Not a hand, just bricks and mortar. Not a living thing, but a lesser shade of light.

"Calm down," he said, ignoring the manic thumping of his heart. "You're too smart for this. And too old."

He wiped his forehead again, but this time his skin felt wet and sticky, much too hot to be a matter of exertion. He imagined his brain tied to a spit, slowly roasted over crackling flames. The idea made him dizzy, nauseous—and just like that, his day was done. After tossing the shovel beneath the cover of the eaves, he dragged himself inside and to his bedroom. Like every evening, before he crawled under his sheets, he turned on the bedside lamp.

For the next few hours his condition only worsened. He struggled against the pain and exhaustion that rendered his head and limbs into lead weights, tied to his body by a length of string. At times, he managed to fall asleep. But the burgeoning fever ruined any hope of true rest, tainting his dreams with maddening repetition—every one of them nightmares of unseen things whispering from the depths of endless dark places.

Before he fell asleep for good, he remembered his mother's favorite warning, saved for long winter nights when the lights were off, and the cold made the house feel like an open tomb. She never bothered with lies about the Boogie Man or Santa Claus to keep him from misbehaving. Instead, she would simply say, "Keep it up and the darkness will get you." Short. Effective. Unforgettable to a boy new to fear and steeped in imagination.

Despite the fire spreading through his brain, he couldn't stop himself from shivering.

* * *

Nicholas's fever burned too fierce for him to think straight. Sweat soaked his pillow and sheets, filling the air with a cloying sweet-sick odor. Through the blinds, storm clouds huddled close, blocking out the sunlight and spilling a sheet of virgin snow into a false dusk.

"Wake up, Daddy!"

He recognized that voice, high-pitched and crooning in his ear, but it took a moment for a name to break through his fevered confusion.

"Sarah?" he said. The name felt strange forming on his lips. How many weeks, or months, had it been since he'd seen her last? Try as he might, the memory remained elusive and the pain of thinking soon forced him to relent. "Did your mother let you in? Is she here too?"

Sarah leaned through the doorway, black hair done up in pigtails, cheeks pinched-red globes. The rest of her features remained dark, imperceptible, her borders blending into the insufficient light.

"No. The door was locked, but I found another way in," she said.

"I'm feeling pretty sick right now. Can you play in your room for a while?"

"But I'm hungry. It's time to eat."

He blinked, rubbing his forehead with the meat of his palm. "Sarah, I—"

He meant to say, "I can't," but the next thing he knew he was standing in the gloom of the kitchen. The stovetop burner coil glowed red beneath a skillet lined by sizzling bacon, with a single, sunny-side-up egg crowning the center. A click to his left alerted him that the rice cooker had finished with its bounty. All the while, Sarah sat at the dining table with her fingers laced upon her lap, face obscured, save for a white glint that might have been a smile.

When he placed a heaping portion of the food in front of her, she bent forward. A snort of air, as if she'd given it a sniff. She poked at the egg with a fork—hard enough to burst the yoke—and then dropped it to her plate with a clatter.

"Happy birthday," she said.

"It's not my birthday."

"I meant happy birthday to me!"

Nicholas steadied himself against the table, trying to hide the scalding guilt her words had made him feel. "I'm sorry, Sarah," he said. "My mind's not what it used to be. Maybe we can celebrate when I'm feeling better?"

She shrugged and stood. Her little legs, off-kilter, skipped in the direction of her room, until the soft thump of her footsteps trailed into nothing. Nicholas, in turn, stumbled to his bedroom and turned the bedside lamp on before slipping back into his bed.

* * *

Silence spread throughout the house, save for the rasp of heavy snow falling off the rooftop. With the blinds closed, darkness smothered Nicholas's bedroom, thick as smoke and looming like a presence. He lay in bed and pretended to ignore it, trying to convince himself he didn't feel it stir, or feel it watching.

It embarrassed him to admit the sensation was petrifying. It reminded him of when he was a boy. All those sleepless nights where shadows brimmed between his bedroom walls, and choking on a pillow was the only thing that muffled the sound of his crying. Screaming did no good. Nicholas's father had left before he was even born, and if his mother ever heard, she never came to check on him. With nowhere to run and no one to turn to, his only choice had been to remain still, to keep quiet, until the morning banished every trace of night. In that way, some things never changed.

From somewhere in the room, he heard a scuffle on the carpet. Nicholas groped for the bedside lamp, but knocked it to the floor instead. His heartbeat strained against his weakness, but even its meaty thumps failed to express the fear that gripped him. When he heard the sound again, closer to his side, he grabbed his pillow and swung it back and forth with all his might.

"Daddy?"

He almost tumbled to the floor, but caught himself in time to collapse back onto the bed.

"I'm bored. Can we play in the dark?" said Sarah.

Her voice roamed about the room from one end to another. Sometimes closer, sometimes farther away. And had he heard her question right, or was his mind playing tricks on him again?

"What did you say?"

"I said, can we go to the park?"

He only realized how tense he'd become when her answer eased him into a calmer state, and his body seemed to melt into the mattress.

"No, honey. It's much too far away. Besides, with the roads still slick with snow and ice, it'd be far too dangerous."

"Awww, fine," she said.

He heard the door open and shut, and the darkness seemed to lessen. Before he fell asleep, he restored the lamp to its table perch and turned it back on, trying not to think too hard about why he even had to.

* * *

Nicholas hunkered in the rear corner of the hallway closet, behind a tall stack of boxes. His mother sauntered through the house, searching for him.

"Come out here, goddamn it!" she screamed.

He imagined the wooden rod gripped between her plump, red fingers, its hum splitting the air with each decisive swipe. His back ached in anticipation, and he covered his face behind crossed arms, a warding sign he hoped would further hide him.

"Even if I don't find you, you can bet the darkness will. It feeds on the fears of wicked little children. It craves it. And when it's had its fill of that, it'll feed on you next, meat, bones and all."

At once, Nicholas recognized the mistake of his hiding place. Before, the dark around him lay vacant and inert. But now it stirred, as if it had become a living thing, caressing him with a feather touch.

He opened his eyes and flailed his arms. A deep moan escaped his throat, but when he recognized the contents of his own living room, he slumped back into the couch beneath him. He didn't know how he got there, but was glad the TV was on because it felt like the dark had closed in while he'd slept. As if it had expanded its borders everywhere, except the wide blue stream of the screen's light.

"Daddy," Sarah said from somewhere in the hall. Her doorway, he guessed, but he couldn't tell for sure. "Can I watch a show?"

"Maybe. If you keep the volume low."

For a moment there was quiet. Then he heard the patter of her footsteps closing in behind him.

"Can you turn the light on, please?" he said. "I don't like the dark."

"Why? What's wrong with the dark?"

"I dunno. I never have. Maybe it's because it gives the monsters a place to hide."

"Silly Daddy." She giggled. "If there *were* monsters here, the light would only make them mad, or nervous."

He smiled. His baby girl had always been clever. Far more clever than he was at that age. Maybe more so than he was now.

* * *

They played Candy Land on the carpet of his daughter's bedroom floor, the only lamp veiled by a thick, black t-shirt to protect his sensitive eyes. He was glad she brought the game because he didn't have anything else that could occupy her time. Just grown-up books, dusty bookcases, and old furniture that filled up a lot of space.

The more he thought about it, the more he realized how much he missed her. Fever or not, he reveled in the comfort of her company, and he wondered why he hadn't thought to ask her over sooner. Not since—

"My turn," she said. She grabbed a card, crinkling a corner. "Ice cream cone!" She squealed and licked her lips. "Can I have some ice cream, Daddy?"

"Sorry, we don't have any."

"Then how about a snow cone?"

The silhouette of her finger pointed toward the window, to the thick white layer of snow covering the glass.

"Sure. Just make sure you don't eat the pink or...yellow stuff—"

His voice slid away, and with it went his surroundings. When he became aware again, he found himself slumped upon the toilet, pants bunched around his ankles. He felt wet below, somewhere between those pallid thighs that didn't quite feel a part of him, so he knew he had gone. But when? He dropped a hand against the toilet roll, but only the cardboard tube remained.

Collecting all his strength, he yelled, "Sarah, I need some toilet paper."

No response.

"Sarah?"

Maybe it was later than he imagined, and she'd already gone to sleep. But somehow, he knew she had heard him. Somehow, he could feel her presence on the other side of the bathroom door, listening in the darkness of the hallway. A broad smile creasing her rosy cheeks.

* * *

The blinds allowed in a feeble glow, exposing the barest hint of shapes against the wall opposite the window. Just outside its range, standing by the foot of his bed, was the outline of a figure. A tall thing, skinny as a pole, with needle fingers held flat against its belly.

Nicholas drew the covers to his chin, twisting and pulling on their edges as if he meant to rip them in half. "Who's there? Who are you?"

It took a few short, careful steps. A few more and then the light revealed it clearer, shrinking it down, widening it, until it bore the diminutive shape of Sarah. She held out something rectangular, wrapped in a white sheet of paper.

"Open it," she said.

"Oh, Sarah, you shouldn't have. I should be the one giving you a gift."

"You gave me life." She grinned, and what little of her face he could see burst with overeagerness.

It reminded him of the broken toys and unwanted knickknacks she used to wrap and give away as gifts. Nicholas usually found himself staring down at a legless horse, or the head of a ceramic kitten, or some necklace missing all its plastic jewels. Whatever was inside this time, she must have also brought with her. He tore a jagged line across the top and held it upside down. Photographs slipped into his hand, a stack thick as his finger.

"Do you like them?" she asked.

He squinted at the topmost one, could see various shades of colors, but nothing clear. Nothing concrete.

"What are they?"

"It's us. Our day together. Daddy-daughter pictures."

Nicholas smiled. "I love them. Thanks, sweetie. Tomorrow, we'll look at them together."

* * *

Nicholas opened his eyes. The clock perched above the doorframe announced the hour: 8 AM. For the first time since he had fallen ill, the room opened up to him, exposing walls and corners, the clarity of its many lines and colors. He sat up in bed, soaking up the pleasure of being well. Savoring the feel and brilliance of daylight pouring through the open blinds.

Like every morning, before he crawled out of bed, he turned off the bedside lamp. He went to the window next. Snow fell, thick and unrelenting, riled by a heavy wind that sent it whipping in all directions. He could see nothing past the perimeter of his backyard fence some fifty feet away, already buried to its upper rails. All that time shoveling the walkway had meant nothing; the storm had likely buried his car by now as well.

He was about to head to the bathroom when the content of his fever dreams returned. Especially of the little girl who'd starred in every one, the details of their lives together filled by that same omniscient source that informed all dreams. He couldn't recall her name, but he remembered that she'd been his daughter, and how he could never quite see her face because it was always wrapped in shadows. He also remembered her gift from the last time they were together, and threw an idle glance to where his dream-self had left it.

Upon the bedside table, a sheet of crumpled printer paper lay curled around a pile of photographs. Confusion rattled in the empty space between his thoughts. It took some coaxing before he could gather the nerve to examine them more closely.

In the first picture, he saw himself standing on the front walkway, holding a shovel and staring at the house. In the next, he lay in bed, an arm draped across his face. Then, he was standing in front of the stove, eyes shut, arms limp and dangling by his sides. Another in bed. One of him asleep on the couch. One in the empty office, sprawled across the carpet. One passed out upon the toilet. Another in bed. And another, and another, and another.

He flung the photos to the ground and shoved a fist into his mouth. His legs scissored against urine threatening to explode from his bladder. There came a sharp knock on the door.

"Did you like my photos, Daddy?" the soft, almost sing-song voice behind it said.

Blackness rippled beneath the door gap, stuffing it up.

"Sarah," he said, remembering her name at last.

"Yes, Daddy?"

"You're not my daughter, goddamn it. I never had a kid. I don't even know you!"

"Oh, Daddy. You really are being too silly." Her giggles lingered, overlapping her response. "Now, no more games, and no more excuses. I'd really like my present now."

The door began to bulge. Tendrils of shadow pushed through the cracks of its edges, licking at the air within the room like thirsty tongues.

Nicholas spun around to face the window. Ten miles separated him from his closest neighbor and twice that to the nearest town—assuming he could find it without following the road. He took a stuttered breath as he threw the blinds aside. Then he jerked the window open and stared into the endless white and searing cold buffeting his face.

The door gave out a sickening crack and toppled to the floor. Without a backward glance, he leaped through the open window, landing barefoot on a cushion of snow. The last thing he heard before the storm swallowed him whole was Sarah, her slow, sad voice singing, "Happy birthday to me," into his empty room.

PAGPAG

THE NIGHT WATCH WAS scheduled for ten that evening, but Jay started his patrol soon as the sun went down. With a newly sharpened *gulok* resting on his shoulder, he ambled down the scabrous road that wound throughout the settlement, ducking clotheslines, skirting refuse, and threading the narrow strips of alleyways between each cluster of shanties. Heavy winds made corrugated rooftops rattle. Plywood walls banged and trembled, and every once in a while, the sound of someone crying bled into the night, adding a somber note to the symphony of violence.

It reminded Jay of his wife Malaya's funeral from two weeks back, shortly after the *aswang* first appeared. All those solemn people huddled around her closed coffin, chanting prayers lost to the howl of buffeting winds. The thought of it put a knot in his stomach and he stared into the sky.

"*Mahal na Panginoon*," he said to the moon, to the stars, to the dust clouds swirling overhead. "Give me justice."

He let hours pass before resting along the eastern border where a wall of buried garbage marked the start of the local landfill. With his back pressed against the wall, he scanned the distance, focusing on the deep shadows that gathered around his neighbors' homes. No sooner had he started than he spotted a figure walking down a parallel stretch of road. He squeezed the *gulok* for reassurance and sprinted to catch up.

"Curfew is at ten, you know," said Jay, falling in step beside the stranger. "Where are you going?"

"Home," said a man's deep and graveled voice.

Jay searched every inch of him, looking for a sign of abnormality. The man wore a hood pulled down over his eyes, his hands thrust into the pockets of his dusty jeans. Added to the scars around his tightly drawn lips, he looked suspicious enough. But Jay had to be sure.

"Remove your hood so I can see your face."

"Mind your own business."

"It is my business," said Jay, grabbing his arm.

The man jerked free and spat a black glob that landed on Jay's shoe. In one swift motion, he yanked his hood back. "*Putang ina mo,* is this what you wanted to see?"

The *aswang's* jaundiced skin cradled the contours of its skull, pulling its features into a scowl. Dark rings surrounded its eyes. Its pupils narrowed and the tip of its second tongue—a slender pink proboscis—slid from its mouth and brushed against its chin.

Jay jolted back. He raised the *gulok* to defend himself, expecting the thing to lunge, or slash at him with nails thick and hard as ivory, like others had done before. Instead, it turned away.

"I have no time to waste on you," it said.

Before it could take a step, Jay kicked its knee-pit, knocking it to the ground. Rage surged inside him as images of Malaya's last moments barreled through his mind: the abject terror in her eyes; the way her mouth almost formed his name before pain twisted it into a scream; and her father looming over her, slurping from the proboscis lodged into her belly.

He swung his *gulok*, catching the *aswang* between the sloping segments of its neck. With each subsequent hack, he shouted, "You want your family? Here's your family!" and, for a time, the sound of metal cleaving flesh and bone pierced the night.

Once it lay dismembered, he dragged the pieces to the pit that lay beyond the southern edge of town. Roiling darkness filled it up; the stench of rot hovered like a noxious cloud above it.

"Please," said the *aswang's* head, its voice now feeble, shrunken to a sigh. "My family needs me."

Jay pinched his nose shut. Without a word, he kicked the parts in where they fell among the low and garbled cries of all the other *aswang* that had come before.

* * *

He returned home before daybreak and found his mother seated by the table. Candlelight washed over her, throwing shadows across the grooves and wrinkles of her sleeping face. He didn't bother to wake her; he simply dropped to the floor and wept into the cotton of her skirt.

"What's wrong?" she said when she woke, pushing at his shoulders to get a better look at him. "Are you hurt?"

"I met an *aswang,*" he said, his body racked by heaving sobs.

"You were protecting us. No one can blame you for what you had to do."

"That's not it."

"Then what? What could possibly be so bad?"

He lifted his head, meeting his mother's eyes for the first time. "It's just... Why them? Why does their love bring them back to their families, but she doesn't return to me?"

"Ah, Jay, you're not thinking straight. What would you do if Malaya did return? Hug her? Kiss her? Bring her into this house and pretend she won't do to you what her father did to her?"

"We never even had a chance to say goodbye."

"Perhaps God is saving you from foolishness," she said, wiping the tears from his cheeks. "You can't handle that burden yet. Two weeks is too soon."

* * *

They woke at sunrise and finished the untouched *pagpag* from last night's meal. The meat had soured in the night and the rice had hardened into clumps, but they ate their share without complaint. It was better than the alternative, when their empty bellies felt hard as stone and the need for food squirmed and clawed like a ravenous beast inside them. Thankfully, those days were few and far between now that Jay had replaced his mother as the family's sole provider.

After breakfast, Jay stood and stretched his limbs. "I should go."

"*Mag-ingat ka,*" his mother said, her expression almost plaintive. "You do what you have to do to come home safely."

"Don't worry. I'll be back before you know it."

On his way downtown, he passed a roadblock where soldiers in ACUs pointed guns and asked him questions: "Where did you come from?" and "Where are you going?" and "Where does your family live?" They shined light into his eyes and checked his fingernails. At the tail end, a man in latex gloves pried his mouth open and, seeing nothing unusual, sent him on his way.

He arrived in Manila's commercial district by late morning. Not long ago, cars would have choked the roads between each stop sign, and sidewalks would have overflowed with pedestrians. But the fear of *aswang* had left their mark on the people of the Philippines. While richer families had fled the country, the majority—Jay's neighbors and those like them—were too poor to travel and hid within their homes, waiting out the crisis behind barricaded doors. Now he could count those spread across a city block on his hands.

In the rear of his favorite shopping center, the buildings and a high brick wall sandwiched a paved alley. A row of bins lined the wall, a few with lids flipped open and their stink spilling out. Before long, he was elbow deep in garbage.

"Get out of my trash, you mongrel!"

He heard a bark of laughter and turned to find Peter—another frequent scavenger among these parts—strolling toward him. Peter scratched the beard beneath his wide grin. What few teeth he had peered above his lips, like black icebergs floating in a pink sea.

"*Kumusta ka*, Jay," he said.

"*Kumusta po kayo.* You almost gave me a heart attack."

"I'm keeping you on your toes, that's all. How's business?"

"There still aren't enough people dining out."

"Tighten that belt, my friend. With Laog overrun and Quezon like a ghost town, I fear the worst is yet to come."

"I hope you're wrong. If this keeps up, we'll starve."

"Look on the bright side! At least there are less of us dogs fighting over table scraps," Peter said, rubbing his hands together like a kid surveying his birthday spoils.

They worked in silence for a while, but memories of Malaya bandied for Jay's attention and he was unable to concentrate on anything else. He remembered the first time he took Malaya on a *pagpag* hunt. A life of scavenging metals and plastics with her father at the adjacent landfill had left her unprepared. The moment she came across a rotted piece of meat—rife with maggots—she hauled herself aside and retched.

Jay kneeled beside her and took her hand. "Have you ever wondered why we call it *pagpag*?" he asked.

She shrugged, wiping the remnant sick from her lips.

"My mom told me it's because we scoop it up and shake the dust off. It's not what we wanted, but it's all we have. We come from dust, we live in dust, and when we die we go to dust."

The memory faded. Jay balled his hands into fists. A ferocious ache coiled like a snake around his heart and standing straight, tilting his face up into the sky, was all he could do to catch his breath.

"Peter, are you still living in that cemetery up north?"

"Of course. It's only the most luxurious space on God's green earth! Why?"

"I've been tracking news of the *aswang* for weeks now, trying to get a better sense about them. Maybe you noticed something while living there that I missed."

"Perhaps," he said, scratching his beard again. "How about this: They're not dead, at least not in the way you might expect. A week ago, before I made camp, I struck up a conversation with a man who had lived in Manila North Cemetery all his life. I asked him how he could feel safe knowing the *aswang* were all around and he just laughed. 'There are no *aswang* here,' he told me. 'The crypts are sealed, the ground is undisturbed, and bones are stacked in the common graves up to the highest brick. Assuming God hasn't plucked those bastards straight from Hell, they come from somewhere, but not here.'"

"So where?"

Peter turned, staring owl-eyed at Jay. "That is a question! I can't say. In the end, only the *aswang* know for sure."

* * *

A nightmare kept Jay from anything like true rest, the same one he'd had every night since his wife died. In it, he relived the evening that Malaya's father returned.

Jay and his family hadn't known better than to welcome him into their house. At the time, the *aswang* were still the stuff of myths and legends, mostly shape-shifting she-devils who lived as women by day, but changed into vicious beasts at night. And Malaya's father had been dead three days. That was key. If it had been longer—a week, a month, a year—maybe they would have feared him and slammed the door in his face. But three was holy. Three was perfection, a sure sign that a divine miracle had taken place.

They spoke with him for hours about his funeral, listing all the friends and family who attended, recounting many of the beautiful things that each guest had said. Afterwards, Malaya's father took her for a walk.

"I prefer we go alone," he said. "To make up for my absence."

They left the house together. Less than a minute passed before Malaya screamed and, by the time Jay had thrown open the door and rushed outside, there was little he could do but watch her die.

He woke with the onset of a groan that refused to rise. Sweat poured from his forehead. He turned to his mother, lying beside him in the cramped quarters of their bedroom. With moonlight punching through their wire mesh window, she looked so small and fragile, her breath straining against the weight of her own bones.

He thought about the question that had haunted him since his conversation with Peter. Where did the *aswang* come from? While no closer to an answer, he was determined to find out. No matter what it took, he had to see Malaya again.

"I'm sorry, Mom. I know you need me, but I need her too."

He touched a part of her hair that draped farthest from the bundle of cloth she used for a pillow. Once he settled down again, he drifted back to sleep and to the nightmare of Malaya's death that never seemed to end.

* * *

Jay had only managed to collect a small bag's worth of *pagpag* the previous day, including chicken bones with a few good bites left, a half-eaten hamburger, and a small roll of *ube* cake. They saved the *ube* cake for breakfast. While its outer layer crumbled at the touch, each wedge tasted sweet and they savored every bite.

"Mom, what would you do if I wasn't around?" Jay asked, after he stuffed the last bite into his mouth.

"Ah, Jay! Don't talk like that. It's too morbid," his mother said, waving her hand as if fanning a bad smell.

"I'm serious. What if I get hurt or, worse, killed?"

"I could go live with Perla and her husband. They wouldn't like it, but we've been friends far too long for them to say no."

"Maybe you could visit *Ate* Perla today? I'm going to be late tonight and I'd like to know you're safe."

"No. I'll wait for you here, like always."

"Please?"

"Am I so old that I can't make my own decisions? You come back and maybe tomorrow we can visit Perla together."

He heaved a sigh and enfolded his mother from behind her chair. She went stiff in his arms, but she didn't pull away. They had never been a hugging kind of family, not when he was a boy, or even between his parents before his father abandoned them for good. Her subtle squirming in his arms felt awkward, but he didn't regret it. He needed something stronger than words for what could very well be his last goodbye.

Though it wasn't his turn for Watch duty, he took his *gulok* with him. By the door, he faltered beside the Polaroid of Malaya, propped up on a shelf. The photo had been taken three years ago by a friendly tourist and given to her as a gift. In it, she was eighteen, her face lit by a full and hopeful smile and framed by long, black hair the sheen of ink.

After kissing his fingers, he pressed them against the photo. "*Minamahal kita.*"

"Be careful out there, Jay."

"I will," he said, and stepped into the morning's warm embrace.

He had already decided there would be no *pagpag* hunt. They still had an emergency supply of rice and, besides, he needed to prepare himself for the day that lay ahead. He went first to the river to bathe. The riverside was an isolated spot, hidden from a housing development behind a row of trees knitted together by their branches. In the distance, the buildings of downtown Manila seemed to dangle from the sky like a faded backdrop.

After stripping off, he dove into the rust-colored waters and settled in. Before each dip beneath the surface, he stared into the sky, calling out, "*Panginoon ko,*" and tried to let the river wash away his fears and doubts. It didn't work. He left with a greater sense of urgency, but nothing more, nothing less.

In the commercial district, he found a discarded plastic bag and shoved it in his pocket. Then he strolled along the near-abandoned streets of Manila, biding his time until the sun went down. He needed the cover of darkness for what he had planned next.

* * *

When Jay returned to town, two members of the Night Watch had already started their patrol. Though they meandered along the road, boisterous conversations and their penchant for singing marked their place around him. He had only to drift between shadows, and pass through alleyways, and he arrived at the pit beyond the southern border unnoticed.

Setting the *gulok* aside, he dropped to the ground and dangled his legs over the pit's edge. Despite the late hour, stars remained invisible and even the watchful moon seemed to shed too little light. It made it impossible to see beyond the black amorphous stain covering the pit's bottom. The whispers from dismembered *aswang* drifted out—like funeral songs or unholy prayers—and he saw it not as a fifteen-foot-wide hollow, but as a portal to damnation.

He didn't want to think about what actually awaited him below, so he took a fortifying breath and gave himself to gravity. The fall was short. He gasped as the darkness consumed him, but soon his feet sank into the muddy ground. For a moment, he imagined hands reaching out to pull him under and severed heads chomping at his legs. He held still, waiting for these figments to pass before trudging through the mire.

Among the chorus of spectral voices, he listened for a single one—the graveled bass of the *aswang* he'd dismembered days before. While hunched low to the ground, he called out, "Do you remember me?" in hopes it would respond. He paced the pit several times, back and forth, before something finally answered.

"Yes, yes, I remember you. Are you here to see my face again?"

"I need your help."

"And why would I help you?"

"You said before you wanted to see your family. I can bring you to them, *if* you show me where you came from."

"My family first or we have no deal."

While Jay didn't trust it to keep its promise, he didn't have much choice. Without the *aswang*, his whole plan failed.

"Agreed," he said at last.

After hoisting the head up and shoving it into the bag, he wiped wet, viscous grime against his pant legs, praying it was only mud. He slung the bag over his shoulder. Then he made divots in the pit wall for hand and foot holds and clambered out to freedom.

The entire time, his wife's name echoed in his mind. Since her death, he'd avoided speaking it aloud, but now the anticipation of seeing her again begged him to break his silence.

"Malaya," he said, and a shiver dashed up his spine.

* * *

With the *aswang's* help, they quickly found its family's home on the northeast side of town. Jay stood in the darkness of an alley opposite the house, letting the head peer from the bag through a gap in their tarp curtains. Candles lit the interior, enough to see a mother pass to and from the bedroom, and a daughter and son playing hand games at the table.

"Has it been so long?" the *aswang* said, its waxen face unmoving, save for the tremble of its lips. "When I died, my children were only babies. Take me closer."

Jay stepped into the road, still within the cover of shadows.

"Closer," it said, its voice choked and desperate.

He took another step, right to the edge of moonlight.

"Closer, closer. Go to the window."

Jay could hardly understand its words; the wet gagging of its throat destroyed enunciation. But he knew the motive well enough, could feel the raw, bestial hunger riding the torrent of its moans.

"That's close enough," he said, barely containing his disgust enough to keep his words a whisper. "Leave them with memories and stories. It's better that way."

The *aswang* said nothing, so Jay closed the bag around it. Once he determined the Watch's position by the sound of their voices, he fled in the opposite direction.

* * *

The *aswang* set Jay on an eastern route along city roads and sidewalks. The light of roadblocks shone bright as beacons in the night and he circled far around them, passing through residential neighborhoods or empty fields to escape their notice. Once in a while, cars would pass, but no one stopped him, not even volunteers of the Watch. For hours, they moved through many cities, and crossed two rivers, until the *aswang* made them rest along the border of Antipolo.

"Are we close?" said Jay, gazing into the bag.

"No, but you must put me down here," it said.

"That wasn't our deal."

"I can be of no more use to you. The farther I am from my family, the more compelled I am to see them. It won't be long before I do nothing but beg and cry for you to take me back."

"But—"

"The doorways between our two worlds are spread across the islands, each one opening and closing according to their time. This one is the closest now. It will remain in place long enough for you to find it and do what you need to do."

Jay placed the bag on the ground. "I want to see my wife. If I call to her, will she come out?"

"Perhaps, but you'd risk much by even trying."

"That doesn't matter. Nothing matters except seeing her again."

"And if you die?"

"Then I die."

The *aswang* laughed, a hoarse rumbling in the back of its throat. "Now I see. Despite the life flowing through your veins, you're one of us already."

* * *

Jay left, following the *aswang's* final instructions. Several miles onward, he arrived at a grove of *balete* trees fanned out in a semi-circle. Their branches spread into a thick canopy of leaves far above him, blotting out the sky. The tendrils of aerial roots along their trunks twined with those of their neighbors, forming a barrier of living wood. In its center was a gap, wide enough to fit a man, but barely. A faint haze overlapped it, much like the illusion of blue streaks seen on distant roads in summer.

He took a stuttered breath. "Malaya? It's me."

No answer came, so he shouted, "Malaya, please come out! I have to see you!"

When that failed, he ventured closer, pressing his lips up to the limit.

"I need you. Come back to me."

The door flickered, revealing for a few scattered seconds a clear view of the hillside that lay behind it. Was it closing like the *aswang* had warned and, if so, how much time was left? One minute? Thirty? Enough to call to Malaya for five or six more hours? There was no way to tell, but Jay did know one thing beyond a shadow of a doubt. If his wife's love wouldn't bring her out, he'd just have to go in and find her.

He braced himself, strengthening his will with more good memories of Malaya. But the moment he made as if to enter, hands appeared, dangling from the center of the door as if anchored to the haze itself. He scrambled to a safer distance. The hands groped at the air, sliding forward to reveal delicate wrists and arms as smooth and thin as bone. A leg shot out next, and then the entire body emerged into the night.

"Jay, where am I?"

"Mom?"

The world blurred beneath the warm, wet pooling of his tears. He tried to speak again, but his tongue felt three sizes too large and the soft moans squeezing from the back of his throat were all that he could manage.

"I saw Malaya," his mother said. "She returned, just like you wanted. She forced herself inside our home and asked me where you were. When I refused to tell her, she said she wasn't an *aswang* like her father, but that God Himself had freed her from the prison of her death."

She shuffled closer. Even in the dim light of the *balete* grove, Jay could see her frailty was false, as if she'd forgotten all her pains and senescence and was just mimicking the motions. Her hands slid behind her back. The muscles of her arms flexed, straining toward a purpose he couldn't see.

"She thought she could fool me, but I saw through her lies. I screamed, 'You're not my daughter-in-law' and ran for the door. The moment I threw it open, she grabbed me by the hair and dragged me back inside. Somehow I escaped. I had to warn you. I had to tell you that home isn't safe anymore."

"Mom, please," he said, his voice vacillating between a whisper and a shout. He held a hand out, fingers splayed. "Don't come any closer."

She took another step, dragging herself to within mere feet from where he stood.

"I was so scared. You were gone so long and I was all alone. But I was brave. See? I'm not as helpless as you think."

"Think about what you're doing. I'm your son, the only family you have left," he said, trying to stall her, to force reason into her brain.

"You think I forgot?" Her lips stretched into a ravenous grin and her pupils narrowed into slits. "That's the reason I came back."

A putrid scent rode the wave of her groaning exhale, even as her second tongue slithered from her mouth like a serpent rising from its burrow. When she revealed her hands at last, nails hung like keratin daggers from her fingertips.

"Mom—"

The proboscis lashed out, hooking Jay's arm, ripping a divot in his skin when it finally retracted. He screamed, more out of surprise than pain, and heaved the *gulok* overhead. His mother charged just as he sent the blade crashing down. While her claws shredded his shirt, barely missing the soft flesh of his stomach, his *gulok* found its mark and sank deep into her skull.

He couldn't bear to see her—thrashing on the ground, howling like a wounded dog—when he brought the blade down again. But by the sixth and seventh time he couldn't look away. He had to be sure to strip away whatever life had filled his mother's counterfeit body, so that her soul could truly rest.

* * *

Seconds and eternity fused into an indistinguishable whole, so much so that when Jay emerged from the doldrums of his mind, he wasn't sure how much time had passed. He remembered little of the journey home, except that memories of Malaya no longer comforted him anymore, having been razed by figments of how she'd killed his mother. Only hours ago, he would have done anything to say one last goodbye; now he didn't know if he could even bear the sight of her.

He arrived at the outskirts of the shantytown by daybreak. Quiet filled the empty streets and alleyways, a tainted calm that reminded him of graveyards, or an ancient battlefield where the bodies of the dead had been left to rot. Whenever a stray voice did slip out from the shanties around him, it felt like an aberration, spectral words spilling from another realm.

A sense of unreality bled into his surroundings when he reached his house. Colors faded, objects distorted with exaggerated proportions, and the ground thumped against his feet as if it had acquired its own heartbeat. He hesitated by the entrance and stared up into the sky.

"*Mahal na Panginoon,* give me the strength to do this," he said and muscled through the door.

The stench of rot assaulted him. In the far corner, Malaya cradled the real body of his mother. Blood pooled around them, was smeared across Malaya's face; her lips and teeth were stained with it, her hands wearing it like gloves.

Vomit burned his throat, flooding his mouth. While he'd believed his *aswang*-mother's story, knowing the details only magnified the revulsion of seeing it for himself.

"Why would you do this?" he said, hunched over, spitting sour bile to the floor.

"I'm sorry!" Malaya shouted. "I'm sorry!"

She pushed his mother's body aside, wedging herself farther into the corner, shielding her face with her arms.

"I'm your husband," he said, pounding his chest with a fist. "I'm the one you loved the most. You should have only wanted me!"

He advanced on her, not caring for the consequences. Even if she tried to rip his still-beating heart from his chest, he wouldn't struggle or even cry out. It would be a mercy, an end to all the pain and confusion glutting up his insides. He stooped and grabbed her arms, forcing them to part, fully expecting her proboscis to thrust into his belly. To his surprise, he found only black tears sliding down her cheeks.

"I don't understand. Why don't you kill me? It's what you want, isn't it? My blood, filling you up to bursting."

"I'm too...full. The hunger's gone, at least for now."

He scoffed, shoved her hard against the wall and backed away. "This isn't how it was supposed to be."

"I never meant to hurt anyone," Malaya said, "much less you and Mom. For days I traveled home, thinking about this very moment. With every step, I swore I'd be a good wife and daughter-in-law, not a monster like all the rest. But there's something else inside me now, a blinding lust beyond anything I could have ever imagined."

"You should have *tried harder!*" he said, stabbing a finger in the air at every punctuated word.

"I wanted to, but I couldn't, Jay. I couldn't." She tilted her head, exposing the soft curve of her neck, wiping the wet from her eyes with violent, careless swipes. "You have to end this. The hunger is already returning. Don't let me spend eternity knowing that I murdered the only man I ever loved."

He squeezed the *gulok* in both hands, testing his strength, his mettle. But he couldn't find the rage that had fueled his long walk home, only a fierce loathing for the thing his wife had become.

"All I have left inside of me is hate. If you make me do this now, it's all I'll ever have for you."

Malaya shivered, as if from a cold only she could feel. Her face squinched with pain and her throat distended. "It's coming. Do it."

"No!"

"Jay, please!"

She clamped her lips shut, but her second tongue struggled in her mouth, disfiguring her face with lines and bulges. Jay raised the *gulok* over his shoulder, tears burning his cheeks.

"This isn't how it was supposed to be!" he screamed, and swung with all his might.

Malaya crumpled in place, her body wracked with spasms. Just to be sure he drove the life from her, he hacked fissures in her skull. When at last she didn't move, and the proboscis hung like a withered, pink vine from her mouth, he dropped to his knees beside her.

"I lied before. *Minamahal kita.* Always."

He brushed her hair so that it covered up her wounds, wiping away the blood and grime until the true brown of her face shone through. Then he closed his eyes and cradled her hand in his own.

"Why?" he said, pressing her hand to his face, pretending it was alive and warm. Pretending it didn't bite into his skin like a worthless lump of ice. "Why do we never get to say goodbye?"

PUBLICATION HISTORY

"A Pocket of Madness" first appeared in *Digital Horror Fiction: Volume 1* (Digital Horror Fiction), 2018.

"Behind the Walls" first appeared in *Cutting Block: Single Slices, Volume 1* (Cutting Block Books), 2017.

"A Thing in All My Things" first appeared in *Urban Fantasy Magazine*, 2015.

"Multo" first appeared in *Apex Magazine* #68, 2015.

"Hollow Skulls" first appeared in *Tales from the Lake Vol. 5* (Crystal Lake Publishing), 2018.

"She Who Would Rip the Sky Asunder" is original to this collection.

"Penelope's Song" first appeared in *The Third Spectral Book of Horror Stories*, 2016.

"So Praise Him" first appeared in *That Ain't Right: Historical Accounts of the Miskatonic Valley* (DefCon One Publishing), 2014.

"The Last Great Failing of the Light" first appeared in *Myriad Lands: Volume 2: Beyond the Edge* (Guardbridge Books), 2016.

"Sleeping Cupid Wakes" is original to this collection.

"Plastic Love" is original to this collection.

"Winter Fever" first appeared in *Shock Totem* #10, 2016.

"Pagpag" first appeared in *Apex Magazine* #89, 2016.

ACKNOWLEDGMENTS

I'M INDEBTED TO DAVID BLAKE, Michael Wehunt, and S R Masters for their insights and suggestions. Before I tossed these stories into the cruel and unforgiving fires of the slush pile, they often crossed their desks first, and came out all the stronger for it.

ABOUT THE AUTHOR

S AMUEL MARZIOLI IS AN Italian-Filipino writer of mostly dark
fiction. His stories have appeared in numerous publications and
podcasts, including the Best of *Apex Magazine*, *Shock Totem*,
Tales from the Lake Vol. 5, InterGalactic Medicine Show, LeVar
Burton Reads, and the NoSleep Podcast. His debut chapbook,
Symphony of the Night, was published by Aurelia Leo.

CPSIA information can be obtained
at www.ICGtesting.com
Printed in the USA
LVHW031141030121
675394LV00005B/447